FLIGHT OF THE
TIGER MOTH

FLIGHT OF THE

TIGER MOTH

MARY WOODBURY

COTEAU
BOOKS
FOR TEENS

Edited by Barbara Sapergia
Cover design and photo montage by Duncan Campbell
Cover painting by Dawn Pearcy/"Close-up Of a Pilot Smiling" by Superstock
Book design by Karen Steadman
Printed and bound in Canada by Friesen's

Library and Archives Canada Cataloguing in Publication

Woodbury, Mary, 1935-
Flight of the Tiger Moth / Mary Woodbury.

ISBN 978-1-55050-364-7

1. World War, 1939-1945–Canada–Juvenile fiction.   2. Tiger Moth
(Training plane)–Juvenile fiction.   I. Title.

PS8595.O644F58 2007   jC813'.54   C2007-901731-2

10 9 8 7 6 5 4 3 2

2517 Victoria Ave.
Regina, Saskatchewan
Canada   S4P 0T2

Available from:
Publishers Group Canada
9050 Shaughnessy Street
Vancouver, British Columbia
Canada   V6P 6E5

The publisher gratefully acknowledges the financial support of its publishing program by: the Saskatchewan Arts Board, the Canada Council for the Arts, the Government of Canada through the Book Publishing Industry Development Program (BPIDP), Association for the Export of Canadian Books and the City of Regina Arts Commission.

To Clair, David, Robert, Ian, Peter and Sean,
who gave me the inspiration and courage to write
about young men learning to fly.

Once you have tasted flight
You will forever walk the earth
With your eyes turned skyward,
For there you have been, and there
You will always long to return.
– *Leonardo da Vinci*

CHAPTER 1
APRIL 1943

Jack Waters sat crammed into the front cockpit of the Tiger Moth, the motor in front of him roaring as they rolled down the runway gaining speed.

"Hold on tight!" Sandy hollered through the Gosport, the speaker slung around Jack's neck.

The bright yellow biplane bumped along the runway, then suddenly lifted. They were airborne! Jack's stomach felt like it was plastered to his throat. Sweat trickled down his neck and back. It was hotter than blazes in the flying suit, helmet and goggles. Sandy had warned him that it was plenty cold when you got up in the air. He was uncomfortable, but he felt like a real flyer.

"Look down!" Sandy shouted.

Jack turned his head and risked a glance. The city of

Moose Jaw lay beneath them, its houses on the grid of streets like houses in a model train set, its cars as small as Matchbox toys.

Jack gulped air like a diver to clear his ears and the roar of the engine rushed back.

Ahead of them stretched the prairie. In the distance Jack spotted grain elevators alongside railway tracks. A miniature train moved across the wide expanse of grain and hay fields. Farmhouses dotted the prairie landscape like spilled sugar cubes.

Jack was flying. Really flying! His mother had finally agreed to let Sandy take him up and it felt fantastic! Sandy, his sister Flo's fiancé, was a flight instructor at the Moose Jaw air base, twenty miles east of Jack's village of Cairn.

From the ground the air looked blue, but when you were travelling in a plane it had no colour. No shape. The propeller turned so quickly that all Jack could see was a whirr and a blur. The solid wooden prop on the flimsy-looking metal, wood and cloth airplane moved so fast it was transparent. He'd been on a Ferris wheel at the local fair, but this was fifty times more exciting.

Soaring over the endless prairie, far from the city, Sandy put the plane through its paces. He banked, rolled and looped the Tiger Moth. Jack couldn't help grinning, even though the metal seat bit into his skin.

Suddenly Sandy pulled the plane into a heart-stopping stall. He dived, banked, rose and did a complete roll. Jack's stomach lurched. The seat belt dug into his shoulders. Sandy laughed, straightened the plane and flew in a circle, heading down and skimming over the fields.

"Do you want to try it?" he asked.

"Sure," Jack gulped. "But not if I have to do fancy manoeuvres."

"Not yet," Sandy said. "Just try keeping her on course."

Jack's mouth dried. Sandy had drilled him on the basics over the last couple of weeks. Jack had even sat up in bed reading the flight manual late at night. But he was still getting used to the pitch and wobble, the shaking and the noise. He spent most of his time with his feet on the ground or on the pedals of his bike or the family car.

"It's a lot to remember, sport. But I'm here to take over at a moment's notice."

Jack breathed as if he was running a marathon. Nothing, but nothing, in his whole life had been this thrilling, this scary. "I'll take it," he said. He took over the controls, with Sandy prompting him from behind.

He concentrated on trying to keep the Moth straight and level. But as soon as he got the rudder centred and stopped the plane from yawing, the nose crept too high. The rate-of-climb indicator reared up and the wings tilted.

The black ball in the turn-and-bank indicator rolled to the side of the dial.

"We're side-slipping!" Sandy called. "Make the corrections."

Jack's toes were scrunched up in his shoes in an effort to nail his feet to the floorboards. His hand on the stick was stiff, his heart raced. His innards cramped.

But he felt terrific.

"Let's try that again," said Sandy. And so it went. Instead of the short flight Jack had been promised, the one his mother, Ivy, had only grudgingly agreed to, he spent the whole morning in the air.

Jack climbed out of the cockpit after the first two hours in the Tiger Moth, feeling as if he'd been pummelled by his arch-enemy, Jimmy Boyle. Sweat trickled down his face and he wiped it off with a freshly ironed handkerchief.

He grinned at Sandy. "That was swell."

"If you're up for it, we'll go again this afternoon."

"Sure thing." Jack felt pulled apart physically and mentally, frightened and exhilarated at the same time.

"Might as well make hay while the sun shines, as my dad always said." Sandy, his tall, muscular frame released from the cockpit, loped across the tarmac to the lounge.

Jack wobbled after him. His legs felt like a sailor's on shore leave. He wasn't sure his body would cooperate if they did much more of this.

The pilots' lounge at the flying school in Moose Jaw was filled with shabby but comfortable furniture. It smelled of stale cigarette smoke and dust. Jack threw himself down on an old brown couch without waiting to be invited. A couple of guys playing cribbage looked up and laughed.

"First flight, eh?" one of them asked. He tugged at his red moustache.

"You must be Flo's little brother," the other one said. "You're from Cairn, eh?" Jack nodded.

"This is Jackie, all right," Sandy said. "Jackie, this is Walter here with the red hair and freckles and the poor devil about to be skunked is Bertie." Both men nodded in Jack's direction.

"He just saw the village of Cairn from a whole new angle. His mother won't hear about that part, though."

"Mums always worry too much," Walter said.

"Yeah," Bertie agreed. "A man needs to learn new things. Builds confidence."

Jack grinned at the word "man." He knew he didn't qualify yet, but he was getting closer. And he liked the sound.

"A little bird tells me you're expecting the call any day, Sandy," Bertie went on. "All of us instructors would love the chance to get to go." Bertie sighed, looking sadly at Jack. "The RCAF keeps us here training the youngsters." He shook his head.

"Are you going overseas?" Jack felt the world shift again, the way he'd felt when the plane rolled. "When?"

"Could be soon." Sandy put his finger to his lips. "But keep it to yourself. I haven't told Flo yet."

His sister wouldn't be too happy about this news.

After lunch in the airfield cafeteria, Jack and Sandy went up again. At one point Jack looked down and saw the Cairn grain elevator in the distance, the clapboard bungalow where he lived with his parents, the untidy caragana hedge and the gravel lane behind it. He chuckled, wishing he could fly low and wave to his dad, sitting on the front porch of the family's main street business, the Waters General Store.

If his dad could only see him now. Jack felt a year older than when Sandy had picked him up early that morning. He had even had the thrill of taking off on this last test flight. He was more in control of the plane and he was more confident too. He could fly this crate. Looking below at his village and the surrounding countryside, Jack felt his chest expand with pride. It was going to be really hard not telling his parents.

andy and Flo took Jack to the movies that evening in the city of Moose Jaw and after that the three of them went to a small restaurant. Jack had buttermilk, a hot beef sandwich and a piece of apple pie à la mode. À la mode meant with ice cream. The pie didn't taste as good as his mother's, but he needed to eat after starving himself most of the day. He hadn't wanted to throw up in the cockpit. Now he was more tired than he could ever remember.

"How do you like flying, Jackie?" Flo asked. "Ready to sign up?"

"Wish I could."

His half-sister looked extra pretty tonight. Her dark bobbed hair shone under the soft lights in the café and her forest green sweater brought out the dark of her eyes. She sat close to Sandy, across from Jack. Flo and Sandy had met at a dance when several of Flo's nurse buddies from the Moose Jaw hospital they all worked in had dragged her out of her room.

At twenty-six, Sandy was a couple of years older than Flo, but they'd hit it off right away.

Just then a gang of Canadians, RCAF student flyers and their girlfriends, came in, the men nodding at Sandy as they passed. Jack knew they were students by the white flash on their wedge caps. One of the students came over to pay his respects.

"Evening, sir. We missed you today."

"Evening, Marsden."

"Heard a rumour you're going overseas, sir."

Flo lifted startled eyes. "Have you heard something?"

Sandy glared at Marsden, who hadn't realized he was letting the cat out of the bag. He mumbled something and left quickly. Probably scared he'd wash out on his next flight with Joseph "Sandy" Sanderson.

"I was going to tell you tonight." Sandy looked sheepish. "Sounds like I'm being shipped out to England soon. But you can't say anything."

Flo's hands gripped the edge of the wooden tabletop.

Sandy dug his cigarettes out of his pocket and shook one out of the package. "I didn't dare hope. I thought if I said anything too soon…"

"It wouldn't happen." Flo let out a sigh as long as a freight train. "What am I going to do? I don't want to sit here twiddling my thumbs in the hospital in Moose Jaw, living alone in a dinky flat, with the war going on thousands of miles away. I've got a couple of friends who are serving overseas as nursing sisters. Maybe they'd put in a good word for me."

"There's lots of work for nurses right here in Canada," said Sandy. "Somebody has to patch up all the student pilots who crash in training."

"There's lots of work in hospitals overseas too."

"I don't want you risking your life." A frown creased Sandy's broad forehead.

"It's all right for you to risk yours?" Jack heard a sting in Flo's voice.

"That's different," said Sandy a bit stiffly.

"Is it?" Flo asked. "Well, you don't need to think I'm going to sit here being the 'little woman' at home."

"But Flo –"

Jack excused himself and headed to the washroom. Sometimes he felt like a third wheel on a bicycle around these two. He wondered if Sandy knew how determined Flo could be. Even if they were engaged, Sandy hadn't lived with her for sixteen years the way Jack had. He admired her spunk. He knew it drove their mother crazy having a daughter so outspoken and independent.

When he returned, Flo and Sandy had obviously made up because they were holding hands and gazing into each other's eyes.

"Your mom and dad have been swell to me," Sandy said

to Jack as he joined them. "I'm going to miss you all. So promise you'll keep an eye on things."

"I will. Thanks for the flying lessons."

"You better not tell Mom. She'd have a fit. Or Dad," said Flo. "He'd be sure to let it slip or tell the whole village."

"Keeping secrets is hard work, Jackie. No sense worrying your mother needlessly, though. In wartime, kids have to take responsibility for their own decisions," Sandy said. "It's hard, but that's the way it is."

"Mom has her reasons, you know," Flo said. "She's been especially protective of us kids because my dad came home a hero and died the way he did." She sounded almost angry.

"What do you mean?" asked Jack. He knew very little about his half-sister's father, the World War I veteran and flyer.

"He was your dad's older brother, right?" Sandy turned to Jack.

The family didn't talk about Uncle Jack, not even Dad, and he usually told stories about everything. There seemed to be a cloak of silence around his uncle's life and death.

"No one's ever told me the whole story." Jack sighed.

"I'll tell you sometime, kiddo. Not tonight." Flo shook her head.

Jack was puzzled, but he knew better than to pursue it.

"Time we took you home," Flo said. "Mom will be worried and Dad will want to know about the flight."

"Better not tell him too much," laughed Sandy.

"Don't worry." Jack drew a zipper across his face. But he knew he'd tell his best friend Wes McLeod. He had to share the news with someone.

Jack Waters, boy flyer.

CHAPTER 2
MAY 1943

A few weeks later Sandy was sent to Bournemouth, England, where he paraded with thousands of others in front of the king and queen. Flo got tissue-paper-thin military envelopes that unfolded and worked as letters too. There were photos in the newspaper. Word filtered back through Sandy's friends on the air base in Moose Jaw that he had joined an active Canadian squadron, the 418th, and begun flying night missions over Europe somewhere, with anti-aircraft weapons ready to shoot them down.

Shortly after Sandy left, Flo came home for the weekend from Moose Jaw.

"Wish me luck, little brother." She carried a small suitcase into her old bedroom, now the official guest room.

"Why do you need luck?" Jack followed her to the door of the small room. It still had most of her school pennants and photographs on the walls. The quilt on her single bed was a pink-and-white pattern. A fluffy stuffed bear sat on the pillow.

"You'll find out soon enough." Flo hummed as she hung up her skirt and blouse and tucked her pyjamas under the pillow.

"Flo, what brings you home on a Friday?" Ivy Waters burst through the back door with a bag of groceries. Jack's mother was a compact woman with pale skin and neat black hair hinting of grey at the temples. "You should have phoned. I haven't anything special made."

"I got a ride with a student minister – a friend of mine is dating him. He was coming out to see Dr. McLeod." Flo, her dark bob slightly untidy from the journey, came out and stood in the centre of the kitchen. She wore a pale blue linen dress with plain black pumps.

"I hope he's a safe driver."

"Oh, Mom, you worry too much."

"I wish you could take a job at the infirmary at our own aerodrome two miles away. You could move home."

Flo had lived in Moose Jaw for the past five years, first while she was in residence training as a nurse, and after she graduated, in a rooming house near the hospital with several of her friends.

"Listen, Mom, I've got something to tell you. I've joined the WD, the Women's Division of the RCAF. As a nursing sister, I could be called up any day. I've come to say goodbye."

"No, Flo." Jack's mother had been running around the kitchen unpacking the groceries, putting on the kettle and getting tea things ready. She wiped her hands on her crisp apron and sat down at the kitchen table. "Why did you do that?"

"I'm not like you, Mother. I can't just stay here in Cairn, or even in Moose Jaw. Here, I'd stitch up accident victims, collect ration coupons and fold bandages."

"Don't do this, Flo. You could be injured over there – or worse. Listen to your mother for a change." Ivy got up and paced the floor. "Good girls don't do this."

"Who told you that?" Flo's voice was angry.

"Who knows what kind of people you'll be dealing with?" Ivy pulled a hankie out of her pocket and wiped her eyes.

"Mom, someone has to take care of the wounded. I have friends who are nursing sisters and you couldn't ask for any nicer girls."

"I can't stand the thought of you risking your life. Leave it to the military men." Jack's mother wrapped her arms around herself as if she was being hit, still clutching the crumpled hankie.

"The world is changing." Flo glanced over at Jack. He was leaning against the wall, trying to stay out of it. "It's time we women got involved in the tough stuff."

Jack shook his head. His sister was one determined lady.

"Women are needed for their skills," Flo said. "If Sandy is fighting for our freedom, the least I can do is join up and do my part. It's not like I'm going into combat. I want to save lives."

Jack started down the hall to his room. The tension in the kitchen was more than he could bear. Maybe he should go and get his dad from the store. His dad, Bill, was a pretty peace-loving guy. He might be able to calm things down.

Instead, he stretched out on the crazy quilt on his bed and stared at all the airplane models he'd built, hanging on threads from the ceiling.

He could still hear the loudest part of the argument. His mother was crying. Flo shouted about how Mom made her feel like a naughty child instead of respecting her decisions. Then a door slammed and there was silence. He figured his mother had gone to see his dad at the store. Flo had probably gone for a walk to cool down.

He waited until the house was still, then walked over to the garage behind the store, where Sandy's black '36 Ford sat under a tarp. Jack pulled the sailcloth tarp off, folded it and put it on the workbench. Then he took the keys off the hook by the door and unlocked the door on the driver's side. He got in and started the car. It started smoothly like it should. But then, it was oiled and in good condition.

"While I'm away I want you to take care of old Bessie," Sandy had said the day he left. "Can you do that? I bought her with my first batch of paycheques from the Royal Canadian Air Force. I don't want you roaring around the countryside, frightening the wild life, though."

"No sir."

"Take her out for a spin every week or so. Change the oil. Check the battery, especially in the winter months."

"Sure thing."

"Rotate the tires every six months or so. Hopefully I'll be back before you have to do that too many times."

Sandy had stood there with his hands in his pockets. He seemed to be weighing his words. "If anything happens…" he paused. "If anything happens to me and I don't make it…"

"You'll be fine," Jack blurted. He wanted to close his ears so he wouldn't hear what Sandy was saying. He didn't want his mind going in that direction.

"If I don't make it home, Jack, I want you to have the car."

Jack didn't know where to look or what to say.

"However, my boy, if I come back, you better make sure there isn't one scratch on this baby, you hear me."

"Yes, sir."

A couple of days later Sandy had climbed on the train going east and left. Flo and Ivy had cried. Bill and Jack had hurried back to the store in case there were customers. That way no one would see if either one of them had tears in his eyes.

F lo left in May to go east for speedy officer's training and orientation to military life. She was being sent overseas to a military hospital in England. One of her former nursing instructors had asked for her.

Jack stood on the platform beside his dad. Flo and his mother were talking.

"I'll write as often as I can."

"I will too."

"Mom, I'm sorry I lost my temper."

Ivy nodded. "Me too. It was the shock of it."

"You've never liked change." Flo said. "I love it – the challenge of it."

"We aren't much alike. I'll send parcels. I hear the food is awful over there."

The train whistle blew.

"Don't forget to feed Dad and Jack too. Hey, little brother, don't get into any trouble while I'm away."

"Thank goodness, he's too young to fly away too." Bill laughed, gave Flo a quick hug and kiss on the cheek. "Some of us have to stay home and mind the store."

Jack gave his sister a hug. "I'll miss you. Mom always made chocolate cake when you came home weekends." While they stood close together, they whispered.

"Is it me you'll miss or the chocolate?" asked Flo.

"You. If it hadn't been for you, I never would have gotten to fly."

"Sandy says you're a natural," Flo whispered. "Keep flying, kiddo."

As the train started to roll, Flo jumped on.

The last they saw of her, she was waving from an open window in the last car. Jack heaved a sigh and headed home.

CHAPTER 3
JUNE 1943

J ack was mowing the grass after school when his mother came hurrying up the street from the post office carrying a familiar-looking tan airmail letter. It could only be from Flo.

His sister had written a lot since she'd left; but sometimes the letters came in bunches. This was just a single envelope. Ivy carried the unopened letter like it was one of her precious china plates.

Some people might have opened the letter right in the middle of the main street. Not Ivy Waters.

She sighed as she sat down on the striped canvas folding chair in the shade of the caragana hedge. She wore a freshly ironed, flowered cotton dress and no jewellery. She opened the letter carefully. Ivy did everything carefully, thought Jack.

He pushed the mower into the garage and hurried over to her, anxious to hear from the "front." With his sister nursing in a big hospital on some rich person's estate and Sandy flying night missions somewhere, Jack paid attention to all the war news that could get through the censor. His dad read all the papers and reported daily as well.

Ivy sat with the letter crumpled on her lap, her face paler than ever. She looked up as Jack came over.

"Sandy's missing in action."

Jack stopped mid-stride. "When? How? Why didn't we get notified?"

"We're not the next of kin."

"He can't be missing. He's a great flyer." He's going to marry my sister, he added to himself. He taught me to fly. He left his car for me to keep an eye on.

"Go and tell your dad."

Jack sprinted along the road and down to the main street. Sandy couldn't die. Jack needed him. He loved his mom and dad, but they were old and stodgy. Sandy had been a real blast of fresh air.

The first Sunday Sandy drove Flo home and stayed for dinner, he'd regaled them with stories of learning to fly when he was only sixteen, in Red Deer, and how he'd signed up with the Air Force as soon as he could, only to end up being a flight instructor for the RCAF in Moose Jaw.

Jack's dad, Bill, sat on the front porch of their store with the Hobbs boys – as everyone called twins Melvin and Arnie Hobbs – veterans of the First World War. Both men were shorter and fatter than Jack's dad, their round faces red from the sun and wind. Retired farmers, they spent their days at the store, the post office or down the street at the Chinese restaurant.

The three men glanced up as Jack came barrelling down the street. His dad, tucking his white shirt into his dark blue trousers, hurried down the steps. "Has something happened to Flo?"

"Flo's safe, Dad."

"Thank God."

"It's Sandy. He's missing in action."

The Hobbs twins blinked and their cheerful faces crumpled.

"Damn war!" Arnie rubbed his bearded chin. Mel shook his head in sorrow.

Dad flipped the sign in the front window from "Open" to "Closed." "How's your mother?"

Jack looked back over his shoulder. "Really upset."

"I was afraid this would happen. Flying's a dangerous business."

"But Sandy was an instructor."

"In a war anyone can be killed." Dad sighed.

"Uncle Jack came back safely."

"But he wasn't the same man afterwards," his dad replied. "Not the big brother I remembered."

Jack nodded. Flo's dad had only lived for a year after the war. He was buried beside Grandpa and Grandma Waters in the Cairn cemetery.

When they got home, they found Dr. McLeod, the United Church minister, and his wife Mary in the parlour with Ivy. They sat on either side of her on the sofa, Dr. McLeod's arm gently touching Ivy's. Their son Wes, Jack's best friend, looked a bit uncomfortable sitting on the maroon upholstered chair with dainty white lace doilies on the arms. The sofa back also wore crocheted covers to keep stains off the upholstery. Only the family knew about the worn fabric beneath the frills.

Jack felt better right away, seeing them there. Dr. Ian McLeod was balding, with greyish-blond hair and ears that turned red when he preached. He still had a Scottish accent even though he'd immigrated as a young man.

Wes was like his parents, tall and gangly, but where Dr. McLeod had light hair, Wes and his mom had red hair and blue eyes that made them stand out in any group.

Mary hurried to bring them all cups of tea. Jack sipped his slowly. They talked about how wonderful young people like Sandy and Flo were. How brave and daring. Then they moved on to talking about the war in Europe and what they had heard or read or seen on the movie newsreels.

Jack glanced over at Wes. He was clearly not happy sitting there.

Ivy looked up at the two boys, her eyes filled with pain. Jack tried to find something to say that might help.

"I was thinking," he said. "Sandy might have gone down some place in France. He can land any plane, remember. And we know there are Resistance fighters in France."

"That's true," his dad said, "and Sandy speaks good French."

"The Resistance could be helping Sandy escape. Or if he's wounded, they could be keeping him safe while he heals."

"That's possible," Ivy said, brightening a little. "I hadn't thought of that."

"Yes," Mary said. "That's a good thought, Jack."

"And we know what a resourceful fellow Sandy is," Dr. McLeod added.

Jack's dad smiled at him. Jack didn't always say the right thing, but this time he'd surprised himself. And helped his mother breathe a little easier.

Jack nodded at Wes and they walked quietly down the hall to Jack's room.

"I'll show you my new model," Jack said.

"Great," Wes said. "You don't have to tell me what it is."

Jack smiled. "Nope. It's definitely a Moth."

Inside Jack's room, the walls were covered with photographs of airplanes and diagrams of flying machines designed by Leonardo da Vinci. And Jack's own drawings of aircraft wings, propellers and engines, all in painstaking detail. A tissue paper-and-matchstick model of a bomber hung from the light fixture in the middle of Jack's room. It swung in the breeze.

"Sorry to hear the news." Wes picked up an old Superman comic and put it down. "I hate what war does to people. It's not just soldiers who hurt. It's all of us."

"I know." Trust his best friend and favourite philosopher to try to say something deep. Good old Wes. "All we can do is hope. Want to help with the model?"

The model parts were scattered on a small table. Without a lot of talk, Wes handed pieces to Jack as needed or helped hold two pieces together so Jack could glue them. As they worked, the plane began to take shape. Jack felt as if the clean lines of the aircraft comforted him as he sanded the lightweight balsa wood.

Sandy and Jack had flown a full-size version of this plane. It was a good plane and Sandy was a good flyer. The best. Jack imagined Sandy in a twin-engine bomber or a sleek fighter plane. He could handle them all.

Finally they were done and Jack hung the fragile model on a thread by the open window.

"The top half of your room looks like the sky over Cairn, Jack."

"Thanks. But these planes will never crash. They're protected by the threads that fix them to the ceiling."

His models were safe, but how did you protect the people you loved? There were no threads strong enough. Are we all as fragile as these flimsy toys? Jack wondered.

CHAPTER 4

The next morning Jack slipped on khaki shorts, T-shirt and runners and tiptoed down the hallway past his parents' room. He grabbed an apple and a thick slab of bread which he slathered with butter and peanut butter, and snuck out the back door so as not to wake his mom and dad.

The Waters family had had a hard day. All the neighbours had gathered. Gallons of tea had been drunk; plates of homemade squares and cookies brought and consumed. His father had been stuck with the clean-up.

Jack hadn't slept well and decided to get an early start for work. His weekend job, at the Elementary Flight Training School two miles away, might keep his mind off Sandy and things he couldn't control or change. Monday he'd be back at school. His parents were still asleep because their general store didn't open until ten Saturdays, allowing them to stay open late so farmers could get into town.

Jack stopped momentarily in the outhouse and then rinsed his hands under the pump in the backyard. The cold water from the cistern chilled his fingers. He wiped his already-tanned hands on the worn pink towel his mother had left hanging over the edge of the white enamel bucket.

The town water truck lumbered by, making an early morning run to the public water station on the road to Mortlach, the next village, ten miles away across the prairie to the east.

What a week it had been. Yesterday the bad news about Sandy had arrived, and only the day before that, he and his family had gone to the graduation ceremony of the latest batch of young Royal Air Force flyers trained at the base. The station band had played marches. People had sung "God Save the King" and the English CO, the Commanding Officer, had spoken.

There'd been a potluck supper afterwards at the church, and everyone in town had been there to say goodbye to the boys who had come into the village for treats, church, socials or dinners. He'd said farewell to the three flyers who had eaten at their Sunday dinner table the last few months. He'd been too busy at school and work to get to know them very well.

He and his friend Wes had eaten scads of food at the potluck.

At six feet, two inches, Wes had to duck when he entered or left the church basement. His reddish hair stuck up in unruly clumps despite hair cream and constant combing. Jack was barely five foot eight and wiry, but he could eat as much as Wes. They'd demolished a plate of fancy egg salad and salmon sandwiches all by themselves.

"We'll be seeing you, Jackie," one of the flyers had said in his English accent, as he waved his new blue wedge cap. "Too bad you can't fly. It's wizard."

Jack had bitten his tongue to keep from telling the smart-aleck Brit that he *could* fly. The young pilots would ship out to Halifax by train the next day. A ship would take them back to England where they would train as bomber or fighter pilots, now that they had their wings, wings they had earned right here in Cairn.

Jack wondered how many of them would make it through the war alive. They weren't as well trained or experienced as Sandy. And Sandy was missing.

Actually, you didn't have to go all the way to Europe to die. A few students had already died in training accidents right here. Jack shuddered, remembering.

J ack climbed on his bike and pedalled through Cairn. His life and his small village had changed so much in the last two years. He turned onto the gravel road heading north out of town and put on the speed. Sweat trickled down his forehead. He wiped his brow.

He whistled "You Are My Sunshine" to try and cheer himself up as he cycled toward the airfield. His job was to help the mechanics keep the airplanes in working order, and usually he did a lot of work cleaning them inside and out. Sometimes he got to work alongside the mechanics. He could manage oil changes and minor maintenance jobs as well.

He'd watched the whole training base being built in the late fall of 1941, including the airfield, hangars, shops and H-huts, and housing for the instructors and staff. Now, two years later, he felt much more mature.

At first, RAF maintenance people had done all the work on the base. Then Jack had made a place for himself – and lots of tips – delivering coffee, cigarettes and snacks from his dad's store out to the construction workers. The money was in the bank in Moose Jaw. Jack was saving for university, although he did buy himself the occasional book or model plane, too.

Finally the RAF had sent all the maintenance and support staff home to work for the war effort in Britain and the station had started hiring local workers. Now Jack's weekend job meant that at last he could get close to the planes, even if he didn't get to fly them.

Jack sped up. If he hurried, Mabel Turner, one of the instructors who managed the Link Trainer, might give him a turn. The flight simulator helped train the student flyers. The Link was fun, pitting Jack's manoeuvring skills against a machine. It helped to keep his senses sharp, helped keep fresh what he'd learned flying with Sandy.

The Link was a small cockpit with stubby wings and it was attached to the floor. It had a radio receiver and all the controls of a plane inside. The instructor sat at a desk nearby and shouted orders over the radio to the pilot crammed into the Link. A guy named Link must have invented it. Jack thought he'd like to meet Mr. Link, ask him how he designed his simulator.

Jack would squeeze into the tiny cockpit. The first time, he'd panicked. The controls of the stick and rudder pedals were very sensitive, and Mabel kept shouting directions through the radio. A slight push moved the stick to the left and sent the left wing down. A pull toward him sent him up into the sky. Mabel had laughed at his inability to move fast enough to correct the right rudder pedal's sharp turn. Sitting at her desk close by, she'd monitored his progress and applauded his successes.

Jack loved machines – his dad's old pick-up truck, the tanker that delivered water to the houses, and most of all, Sandy's black '36 Ford parked in the garage behind the store. Sandy had let Jack drive the Ford a couple of times before he had shipped out for the war.

A couple of meadowlarks sang from a telephone wire. Two Tiger Moths flew overhead and a formation of Oxfords, single-engine advanced trainers from the Moose Jaw Service Training School twenty miles to the east, streaked across the sky further up. A flock of ducks rose from the slough by the gravel road.

When Jack was young, the sky over Cairn was quiet as a winter morning. Now the drone of airplanes or the stutter of a stalled engine pulled his eyes up every time he went outside. Once he'd watched as a Moth's engine banged and stopped in the middle of a manoeuvre. The plane dived to the ground and exploded, killing an instructor and a student pilot. There were already four student graves in the Cairn cemetery.

Jack pedalled faster.

An early morning breeze blew over the miles of waving wheat and threw dust from the edge of the road into his face. He blinked and wiped his forehead with the back of his hand. His dark hair was combed flat, with a part on the left side. His ears stuck out, which he hated, but the village barber trimmed his hair too close to his scalp no matter how much Jack asked him not to. At least he had no trouble keeping his thick glasses hooked on his head. The glasses protected his grey-blue eyes from the dust, gravel or midges as he walked or rode across the prairie of southern Saskatchewan.

They were also the reason he'd never be a fighter pilot.

Jack's bike responded to the power in his muscled legs. He wished for another growing streak but figured at sixteen he was probably as tall as he was going to get. But he had a lean, strong frame and could run faster than any of the boys in Cairn or Mortlach.

Before him stretched miles of clear sky and beneath that sharp line of pale blue on the horizon lay prairie grasses and forage crops as far as the eye could see. Overhead, tree swallows dived and swooped like miniature airplanes, hunting for insects. A lazy hawk circled high above and brilliant sunlight shone on Jack, warming him more than the woodstove in the kitchen.

Funny, he'd never thought about landscape until the British flyers commented on how flat and boring the prairie was compared to the green hills and valleys and gracious gardens of Britain. Sometimes he wanted to yell at those young airmen with their funny accents to go back home if it was so wonderful there.

He'd stick with miles of sky and prairie grass.

Dust hung over the gravel road. Someone in town had been driving out this way awfully early. It wasn't hunting season, so who could it be? It was too early for Boyle Transport to be out. Old Jerry Boyle usually got drunk on Friday nights, so he'd be sleeping it off in his ramshackle house on the other side of the tracks.

Up ahead Jack spotted three huge blue-black crows feasting on a dead animal in the easterly ditch close to a clump of wolf willow. He was about to pedal over to the far west side of the road to avoid the sight when he heard a whimper. It was coming from the chaos of screaming and strutting birds.

"Get out! Get the tarnation out of it!" he shouted at the crows as he pulled up beside the mess. A smallish black bitch with thick, matted hair was curled loosely as if ready to feed her puppies, her pink belly exposed. Flies clustered. A pungent rotten smell rose from the corpse.

Jack bent to take a closer look. A bloody hole the size of a silver dollar was drilled into the dog's head. Had to be caused by a shotgun blast.

Tossed under the bushes a step or two further on lay a lumpy gunny sack. Jack grabbed the top of the rough bag, pulled at the worn knotted rope tied around it, breaking a nail as he tore the sack open. The odour of animal sweat, fear and death assailed him.

A fair-sized black puppy with a white flash on his chest and oversized white paws scrambled over Jack's hand and fell to the ground, squatted, piddled, picked itself up and tumbled further under the bushes. Jack opened the sack all the way. The three other puppies inside were already stiff and cold.

Jack dropped the sack quickly, lurched to his feet and brought up his breakfast in the ditch. Then he set about rescuing the remaining pup.

"Come on, buddy." Jack crouched beside the road. "I won't hurt you." He reached into his pocket for the crust from his sandwich and held it toward the shivering animal. "You're safe now."

The pup stumbled out of the bushes and half-rolled, half-waddled over to the outstretched hand. Jack cradled him in his arms as the puppy gulped the bread down.

The crows screeched, stretched powerful wings and paced back and forth like angry vultures waiting for their chance. They had retreated only twenty feet or so to the broken-down roof of a rotting wooden grain shed.

Jack placed the puppy in an open cardboard box fitted inside his black metal bike carrier. He took his work gloves from the box and yanked them on, his mother's constant warnings about germs and dirt echoing in his head. He dragged the dead dog off the road and hauled the sack with the three dead pups back to lie beside her. Then he broke several branches from the brush and laid them gently over the dead animals. Dewdrops on the green mat shone like pearls in the bright sun.

The chorus of crows prompted him to pile more loose vegetation over the corpses. He tried not to think that the crows could shift it away as soon as he left.

He heard whimpering and turned to see the puppy, paws hooked over the side of the box, struggling to climb out. Jack picked up the orphan, who wiggled and licked his hand, and brought him over to where the dead dogs lay.

For a moment the sounds of planes, honking geese and the raucous crows faded. The air stilled. Jack sighed and tried to find the right words for a prayer. "For all the senseless killing in this world, God, we ask forgiveness. Buddy and I leave these your creatures in your hands. That's all we can do. Amen."

So the dog's name was going to be Buddy. Jack hadn't known until he said it. Holding that warm, wriggling body close to his chest made tears spring to his eyes. In the midst of all the bad stuff in the world, here was one small ray of sunshine. Jack knew what he wanted to happen. He just wasn't sure it was possible.

CHAPTER 5

J ack put Buddy back in the carrier box, turned his bicycle around and headed home. He was pretty sure whose old dog he had just covered with branches. Cairn wasn't that big a place, only about 250 people nestled together on six side streets and four avenues. It was far smaller in area than the flight school. Older too, built in the 1880s. The Waters family had been there since the turn of the century.

Cairn sat beside the main east-west Canadian Pacific Railway line. Most of Cairn's citizens were pretty decent folk, as far as Jack could tell. There were a few drunks, a few ornery folk, and a couple of people who didn't have much common sense according to Jack's dad. This pup had come from one of the problem families, Jack figured.

The Boyles had a pack of black lab-terrier mix dogs and lived the other side of town on Pasqua Street, just down from the train station. Their neighbours, the Nelsons, favoured border collies that also ran loose, chasing cows, messing with gardens and scaring cats. Folks knew enough not to bother the Boyles or the Nelsons. The young guys in both families took offence easily, and liked fighting and drinking too much.

Their unpainted houses were a disgrace, Jack's mother said, and their kids ran wild like their dogs. Instead of flowers and neat gardens, dismembered cars and trucks decorated their yards. Jack's mother shook her head over them. Maybe cleanliness wasn't next to godliness but in his mom's mind it sure was close.

Being cantankerous seemed to hold the Nelson and Boyle families together. Jack had sure had enough run-ins with Jimmy Boyle, the youngest of the boys, and his best friend Pete Nelson – or, as everyone called him, Repete, his father being the original Pete.

Jimmy Boyle was a bully. Repete imitated him.

Jack was strong and fast and Wes had been the tallest kid in class, so they hadn't been bothered as often as some kids. Then Jimmy and Repete had quit school after grade ten and life had calmed down. Jack figured this pup was one of the Boyle-Nelson breed.

He pedalled on. He had to talk his mother and father into letting him keep this pup. His grandpa Waters had been a dog person, but ever since he'd died of a heart attack in 1937 there hadn't been a dog around the place.

Grandpa's dog Spike had given up after his master had died of a massive heart attack. He'd stopped eating and Jack figured he'd died of a broken heart. He was buried in the yard under the caragana hedge. Jack had been ten at the time and had thought the dog should have been buried in the family plot in the Cairn cemetery. His dad laughed and made it one of his stories to pass out to customers like liquorice twists.

Now Jack was older and knew you couldn't bury dogs in a people cemetery.

He steered with one hand and kept the pup calm by petting him and talking to him. "We'll see if we can't give you a home, Buddy. Dad won't be a problem. It's Mom we've got to win over." He'd have to promise to walk the dog, probably build Buddy a doghouse, and train him.

Maybe a dog would help his family keep their minds off Sandy being missing. Help them keep up hope. Help keep up the picture of Sandy in France, being helped by the Resistance fighters.

"If I could, Buddy, I'd go find him myself."

Jack knew the Royal Canadian Air Force would take seventeen-year-olds on as "boys." He wished he could go right now. He wanted to help end the war so Flo and Sandy could come home. If he were old enough, he'd go. Mom would be furious. But all the recruitment posters pleaded for the young and able to join the armed forces. He was young and able. He was just a year too young. That's what came of skipping Grade Four. Some of his classmates had already signed up and left. The more he thought about it, the faster he pedalled.

Jack couldn't be a pilot because of bad eyes, but there were lots of things a skinny, compact guy with thick glasses *could* do. Even if he wasn't the biggest guy in grade eleven, he was the smartest in Math and Science.

Jack kept his love of planes and flying to himself.

His mother hated flying and planes with a passion. After all, her first husband had been a flyer, and he had died. But not in a plane, Jack knew that much. His uncle Jack Waters, dad's older brother, had died shortly after coming back from the First World War, leaving Ivy on her own. Ivy had Florence a few months later in 1919. Then Bill and Ivy had married in 1924 when Flo was five. That was all Jack knew.

Jack had watched his mother one morning as she hung out the sheets. They heard a plane engine, then silence, and then the sound of a crash invaded the peace of the early spring morning. Ivy had grabbed the laundry basket and hurried into the house without a backward glance.

Jack stopped in the lane behind his house. He shook his head. Maybe it was a good thing he was too young to go and fight. With Sandy and Flo gone, someone had to stay home and mind the chickens, as his dad said.

"Come on, Buddy, Mom will have had her second cup of tea. I hope the news on the radio is good. Dad says the tide has turned and we're winning more often." He wheeled the bike toward the house.

His mother appeared at the open back window. "Jack? Did something happen at the airfield? You're not sick, are you?"

"I'm fine, Mom."

Ivy Waters burst out of the house, the screen door banging behind her. Flies, fleas and all unsavoury or germ-ridden creatures were banished from Ivy's house.

"You didn't lose your job, did you?" She watched as he propped his bike against the white clapboard house.

"I'm fine, Mom." Jack rescued the wriggling pup from the carrier, clasped it in his two hands and turned to face his mom – small, worried, wearing her crisp, clean, flowered housedress.

She had a smudge of flour on her nose. "I was making cookies to send to Flo in my next parcel," she said.

"Look what I found."

CHAPTER 6

"You can't bring that dog in the house. It's dirty, probably has fleas."

"He's just a puppy, Mom. He's harmless."

"I've never liked dogs," his mother said. Her face looked tight and her eyes dark. "I don't trust them."

"But…"

"Besides, we don't need any more chaos in our lives, Jackie."

Jack stared at his mother. He didn't know what she was referring to. Was it the war, Sandy missing, the idea of a dog? "What's the matter with dogs?"

"A dog is the last thing I need after what's happened." She pulled the creased and crumpled airmail letter out of her pocket. "What if Sandy dies? What then?"

His mother had been carrying the letter with the bad

news about Sandy around with her ever since it had arrived. Did she think that holding on to it would save him?

Ivy Waters didn't even look at Buddy. She turned and walked into the house, her shoulders hunched like an old woman's.

Jack stood stock-still. He chewed his lip. He felt as if someone had kicked him in the stomach. He was a thoughtless kid. He didn't understand anything. The dog wiggled and licked his elbow. Jack left the pup in the carrier and followed his mother into the house.

She sat in the spotless kitchen on one of the brightly painted wooden chairs. A plate of fresh oatmeal cookies sat on the table beside her. Her pale hands clutched the fruit bowl in the middle of the table as if it were a life preserver. The letter lay on the table like a burning coal on an open hearth.

"I'm sorry," Jack gulped.

Jack knew what the letter contained. Flo said that her dear friend (Sandy) had flown somewhere (probably France) to drop supplies (for the Resistance). Jack read between the lines of his sister's self-censored letter. His plane hadn't come back. She was hopeful – she'd nursed one flyer who'd been rescued, and he hadn't even been able to speak another language (French), unlike her dear friend who'd grown up in a bilingual home.

Jack picked up the letter and gently ironed it with his hands, smoothing the wrinkles. He read it again and munched on a cookie.

Ivy began to polish the kitchen table with a damp crocheted cloth, even though there wasn't a speck on it.

"Sandy will show up, Mom. He's a pretty smart guy."

"You should phone Harold if you aren't going in to work, Jack."

"I will." He placed the letter on the small cherry wood table under the oak wall phone.

"Take that dog down to the store. Maybe your dad can find him a good home."

"Why can't we keep him? His mother's been shot. I don't know why they shot the mother. Buddy's an orphan."

She shook her head. "An untrained pup is a load of work."

"I'd train him," Jack said. He ached to tell her about Buddy, but she turned away from him and lifted her bib apron down off a hook, pulled it over her head and knotted the ties tightly behind her. She moved through her kitchen in a circular path as if it were a prison cell. The doors to the parlour and bedrooms were closed. Ivy's universe was small and controlled.

Jack tried once more. "I'd take care of him, Mom."

"You're too busy to take care of a dog and I've got enough on my hands."

"I'd build him a doghouse. He'd live outside."

"No, Jack. We are not going to let things get out of control around here, not if I can help it." Her face was flushed, her eyes blazing. She grabbed the watering can and pushed past him out to her garden.

Jack followed her out and patted the pup in the carrier. "Sorry, Buddy. I guess our timing was bad."

He rode down the block to the store. Ivy had him worried. His solid, predictable mother, the one he'd known before the war, had disappeared. He wanted her back.

The Waters General Store was on Railway Avenue, the main drag of the village, next to the small brick post office and down from the drugstore. The larger and more impressive Cairn General Store and Dry Goods was further down the block beside the Chinese restaurant and the garage with its one gas pump. The two-storey, four-room school and the United Church were up the hill.

Cairn's best feature was its hill. It wasn't every prairie town boasted a hill.

But Jack's dad said that Cairn's hill wouldn't be considered a hill in Alberta. Bill had been to the Rocky Mountains twice. He'd taken Ivy on their honeymoon. "Cairn's hill is a glorified mound, an oversized anthill," he'd said.

Jack didn't care. He liked their hill. The village had a few birch and poplar trees and enough of a slope that you could sled down the hill in the winter, or catch a lift behind horse-drawn carts by gliding on your rubber-soled boots on the ice. Parallel to Railway Avenue ran the Canadian Pacific Railway tracks and on the other side of the tracks stood the tall green grain elevator inscribed with the Ogilvie sign and the brick-red clapboard CPR station with its new roof.

Jack stroked the puppy as he rode slowly down the street, going back once more in his mind to happier times, trying not to think about Sandy dead or a prisoner of war.

Was he dead? Jack shuddered. He pulled away from that thought faster than a lone deer from a pursuing coyote.

Jack patted the pup's head so hard Buddy woofed.

CHAPTER 7

The bachelor twins, Arnie and Melvin Hobbs, sat in their regular places on two wooden captain's chairs on the front porch of the store. They wore their usual old suit trousers with wide-cuffed legs, held up by suspenders and a belt. Their work boots looked dusty and worn.

Arnie wore a crumpled straw hat and sported a ragged grey beard on his weathered face. "Well, if it isn't Jackie Waters," he said. "What have you got there?"

"Didn't know you had a dog," Melvin chimed in. "Where'd you get it?" He blew his nose on a blue cowboy hankie and lifted the stained grey fedora perched on his bald head and smoothed his pink skull.

"I found Buddy in the ditch on the road to the base. His mother had been shot in the head and there was a sack with three dead puppies, and this little fellow."

Arnie nodded. "We know who in town has black dogs."

"Thought I heard gunfire earlier this morning," said Melvin. "Those Boyles use their guns too dang much."

"Don't care if I never see a gun again," Arnie said. "The Great War chased away any love of guns we ever had, right Mel?"

Mel reached over and patted his brother's arm.

Inside, Jack could see his dad waiting on Mrs. Nelson, Repete's grandma. He slipped in quietly and took a great swig of store air into his lungs. There was something reassuring about this place. He'd grown up playing blocks on the floor, surrounded by the comforting smells of the pickle barrel, the flour bins and the tall glass jars with the strong, molasses-tasting hoarhound toffee, liquorice twists, sweet and sours and sugar sticks. He liked the cool and musty air, the dark wooden panels, the worn pine floors and the crowded shelves. He moved to the back of the store by the buckets of nails, screws, nuts and bolts.

He leaned against the rickety ladder they used to fetch goods from the top shelf, waiting.

"Can you deliver these this afternoon?" The old woman peeled a couple of dollar bills off a little stack she had in her leather purse. "Young Pete and his friend Jimmy Boyle have landed jobs working in Moose Jaw on construction. They wanted jobs at the air base, but they didn't have any luck."

She stared fiercely at Jack.

"That's too bad," said Bill Waters.

"They barrelled out of here really early this morning in an old truck Jimmy bought for a hundred dollars from a farmer. Took old Boyle's favourite dog. Not that she's much use now that she's lame. Said they wanted to do some gopher hunting. Then they'd head to the city to look for rooms." Jack waited for the old lady to take a breath, but she went right on. "So many people are moving to Moose Jaw, it's a wonder anyone's left in the smaller places."

"Jack's got a job at the air base, part time," Dad said. "Why aren't you out there, son?" They headed toward the front of the store.

"I didn't make it this morning." Jack pointed through the screen door to the puppy sitting in the carrier basket outside. "I got waylaid by that little fellow – whimpering in the ditch."

"Looks like one of the Boyles' pups," reflected Mrs. Nelson. "Their old bitch tangled with our collie and threw a bunch of pups a while ago. They usually drown them, seeing as we've enough dogs running around. Where'd you find him?"

"I guess he was lost." Jack didn't want to tell the whole sad tale to Mrs. Nelson. It wasn't her fault.

"I could bring these groceries over right away," he said. He walked out onto the porch.

"I'll be home in half an hour," said Mrs. Nelson as she headed down the steps to the dusty main street, leaning heavily on a cane made of shellacked diamond willow with a rubber foot to stop it from sliding.

The brothers nodded as she passed. Arnie was down by the bike, patting the pup. "He's a solid little fellow. Must be about eight weeks old or so. Hefty, too. Well over five pounds, probably the strongest of the litter. What do you reckon, Mel?"

"He'll be a big dog. Look at his paws."

Jack went down the steps and brought the pup up to the porch and stood by the door. He wanted to keep this pup so bad he could hardly swallow.

"Mom wants me to find the dog a home."

"What did she say?" Jack's dad asked, standing by the screen door.

Jack told him. "I'm afraid I really upset her. I didn't mean to."

"This isn't about the dog, Jack. It's about Sandy and the war and the accidents around here with young fliers." Bill Waters stood in the shade behind the screen door. "Ivy's always been a worrier, but now it's worse."

He sighed and walked back across the floor of his store. He closed the flour bin, tightened the lid on the sugar, wiped his hands on his canvas apron and sat down in a captain's chair by the unlit woodstove, his legs stretched out in front of him, his long, pale fingers massaging his rarely lit pipe. "I should probably close up and go home, see how Ivy's doing. I'll deliver Mrs. Nelson's groceries on the way." His father motioned Jack inside with the dog.

Jack stepped back into the store, his eyes blinking from the darkness of the interior. "I really want to keep this dog, Dad."

"You better phone Harold at the maintenance shop and tell him you'll be late."

"I'll do that in a moment."

"Now, tell me about the dog."

Jack told him. "I didn't have a chance to tell Mom how I saved Buddy's life. If I hadn't been going down the road when I did, he'd have died – suffocated or something. I feel responsible for him now."

"I can understand that." His dad nodded.

"But Mom had Flo's letter in her hand. She'd been reading it again and making cookies. She said there was no way she'd let me keep a dog. She didn't trust them. Then she said something about chaos."

"One thing you don't know about your mother, Jack. She was bitten by a black dog when she was a little girl growing up in Arcola."

"But Buddy's just a baby. We'd train him."

Bill Waters smiled. "Ivy wouldn't let Spike in the house and he was my dad's dog."

"I always wondered why the dog had to sit in the yard." Jack remembered Spike whining pitifully, sitting by the pump.

"My dad didn't like leaving him outside either. But it kept the peace."

Jack perched on the other captain's chair, holding Buddy on his lap. He wasn't built like his dad, long and lanky. He was shorter, like his mom. Everyone said he looked like his Uncle Jack, who'd flown with Wop May, a flying legend and a Canadian prairie hero.

"The least we can do is get the wee fellow well equipped." Dad took the pup in one arm and walked behind the counter and over to the section with pet supplies. He chose the smallest collar, a leash and a couple of bowls and brought the dog back to Jack. "Hold him while I make a hole in this collar so it'll stay on."

Bill went to his workbench in the back room and came back shortly with a new hole drilled for the buckle in the small leather collar. He wrestled with the pup, finally doing the collar up and attaching the leash. Jack put the puppy down. Buddy promptly squatted and peed on the wooden floor.

"You'll have to train him."

"I know."

His dad filled one bowl with water and another with dog food and put them down on the floor. Jack mopped the floor.

"Why don't you tie him to the front stoop?" Bill cut a ten-foot length of half-inch rope and handed it to Jack. "I'll try talking to your mother. It may take a while. You watch the store. And don't get your hopes up, Jack."

"I won't." But he knew he would. Buddy was his dog.

Jack tied the pup up outside and washed his hands in the back room before he phoned the airfield and told Harold why he hadn't gotten to work on time.

"Why don't you bring Buddy out to meet the new students?" laughed Harold. "These kids are so young and lost they could use a little cheering up. As usual, I can't understand a word they're saying."

"I have to watch the store for a couple of hours. I'll be out after lunch."

"Good."

Jack was about to hang up when Harold shouted into the phone. "Don't forget to bring Buddy."

The puppy yipped and yapped as Jack hung up the receiver. Jack climbed the ladder that slid on a track along the high shelves to put away some tins his father had left out on the counter. Before he could get down, a farmer came into the store.

"Where'd you get the dog, Jackie?"

They didn't need a weekly newspaper in Cairn – they had the Waters store. Jack wondered if people really came to shop or just to discover what was going on in town.

CHAPTER 8

Jack reached the guardhouse shortly after one o'clock and showed the guard his civilian pass with his photo on it and the typed note with his job description. The new Royal Air Force boys were on parade in the square, marching in precise formation in their blue uniforms.

"They don't look any older than you, Jackie," said the guard. Then he did a double take as Jack rode through the gate. "You smuggling a pup onto the base?"

"Harold wanted me to bring Buddy – to show the guys in the maintenance shop." Jack told the guard his story. "Can I take him in with me?"

"Don't know any rule against it." The guard went into his little house and back to his reading. Jack had been inside one rainy day. The guy must have had a two-foot-tall stack of comic books.

Jack and Wes each had a pile of comics themselves. They saved up to buy them whenever they went into Moose Jaw, then traded back and forth. Some were so dog-eared they hardly held together. Superman was Jack's favourite, because he flew into Metropolis and rid the city of the bad guys. Jack wasn't any superman, but he knew he was hooked on flying.

Jack suspected he was too old for comics, but some nights, after studying algebra or chemistry, writing an essay or reading Shakespeare, he liked to give his brain a rest. As far as he knew there wasn't any rule against it, as the gatehouse guard would say.

Jack cycled over to Hangar Number One where Harold stood by the door holding a dingy white mug of coffee and talking to Angus, his second-in-command on the maintenance crew. Harold was beefy like a football player, with no neck to speak of, while Angus had a paunch that hung over his leather-belted work pants.

"What's this, then?" asked Angus, running his hand through his thinning brown hair. "Where'd you pick up this wee laddie?"

"Tell him the story, Jackie," Harold said, "but I've got to get back to work. And I've got lots for you to do. Poor old 3070 caught a duck in its propeller and fuselage. Start with that. Clean it out." He walked off. "Oh, and tie the dog close to the repair shop. I'll keep an eye on him. Angus can show you what to do."

Angus didn't seem in a hurry as Jack told about the rescue. Angus had a border collie himself, back in Edmonton, that his brother was keeping for him, and he gave Jack all sorts of tips about raising a good dog.

"Border collies like to take care of a group, a herd, a bunch of things, preferably sheep. But they'll herd *you* if you let them. Train them to take care of things, and they're happy as clams."

Jack sighed. "I don't think I can keep him."

"Wish I could help you out." Angus led the way to the tractor at the far corner of the shed. "Rev this fellow up and haul 2804 and 2805 out on the tarmac and give 'em a wash. Get the duck out of the works on 3070. Then fill all these babies with gas so they're set to take off with the new blokes."

Jack whistled as he started up the tractor, headed down the centre of the hangar to the far end and located 2804 and 2805, spattered in mud, as if whoever landed them had driven through the swampy area at the end of the west strip.

Tiger Moths were an easy plane to fly – sometimes too easy, Sandy had told Jack. Young pilots became overconfident and didn't slow down enough, or they didn't get the nose headed into the wind when they came in to land. Most said they were hard to land. Jack hadn't gotten that far. Sandy had landed the plane when he'd given Jack that day of lessons.

He was grateful for all the flying tips he'd picked up. If a fellow kept his ears open, he could learn a lot around the base. And if he could get through the work on time, he would ask Mabel for a half-hour on the Link Trainer. He never got tired of that. Mabel, the best instructor on the base, knew how Jack longed to fly. Harold and Angus wondered why Jack liked to "play" at flying, but Mabel understood why he showed up in the strange circular Link room with its domed ceiling representing the sky.

Jack hooked the towing cable onto the front of 2804, ready to haul it outside through the open hangar doors. Thank goodness there wasn't a strong wind on the runway, or he wouldn't be able to do this on his own. Small birds twittered and flitted back and forth like tiny kites in the massive struts and beams that held up the hangar roof.

Ever so carefully, Jack drove the tractor with the yellow biplane trailing behind it through the massive doors of Hangar One.

He remembered watching this hangar being built. The foreman of the construction crew, who bought coffee from Jack when he used to cycle out to the base, saw he was interested and taught him things he could never have learned in school.

The guy had told him that this was by far the biggest construction job Canada had ever been involved in. "After this we'll be a world power, Jackie boy," he'd said. "The British Commonwealth Air Training Plan will put Canada on the world map, you wait and see. There's nearly a hundred of these aerodromes across the country, and I helped build the prairie ones."

Jack had rarely seen anyone so proud of what he was doing.

"I may not get any medals for this, but I'll know when we win the air war that I did a good job. If a man can say that about his work, he can die happy."

Jack had never forgotten the guy's enthusiasm. He himself would never fly a fighter plane either, but maybe helping at the airfield was enough. He towed the beautiful little plane outside.

Buddy barked and whined, so Jack jumped down and ran over to fetch the dog and tie him up by the first light standard on the field. Then he jogged back to the tractor and towed the biplane to the left side of the tarmac. Buddy barked his encouragement.

He climbed up into the front cockpit first and tidied it. He hung his head outside as much as he could, with the Perspex canopy pushed right back. The inside reeked of old sweat, oil, gas and metal. A crumpled Chiclets box and a wadded tissue curled on the floor.

Jack took a damp rag and washed down the controls, cleaning the windows on the dials, wiping down the speaker tube, the metal student pilot seat, even the rudder pedals on the floor. Thank goodness the last user hadn't barfed. He'd had to clean that up often enough.

The cockpit clean, Jack inserted himself, like a sausage in a skin, into the front seat. It was a tight fit. How on earth would a bigger guy squeeze in, let alone be able to move? A tall black metal rod, the control stick, sat between his legs. The left and right rudder controls were on the floor at his feet. There were several gauges – for oil pressure, airspeed, turn coordinator, compass, and altimeter. The throttle was to his left.

Suddenly he was back in that day with Sandy, roaring down the runway, then lifting into the bright sky. The little biplane had rattled and groaned, the wings tipped, and the ground sped by, and he was enthralled by the wonder of seeing forever and soaring free of the ground. That day would stay with him for the rest of his life.

He cleaned out the instructor's cockpit, slid to the ground and went for the hose. He took a side trip over to Buddy, gave him food and water, and played with him for a moment. The pup rolled and wiggled and panted. He licked Jack's hand, his pink tongue quicker than a slippery, fresh-caught fish from Thunder Creek. Somewhere inside, Jack felt like ice was melting. He hugged the dog and decided it was time to get back to work.

An automobile roared up and came to an abrupt stop. Buddy trembled, anticipating trouble. Four English LACS – Leading Aircraftsmen, or Lowly Air Crew as the village called them – spilled out of the clunker, a '36 Chevy with its roof gone, that the students seemed to pass down like a used suit of clothes. Jack couldn't imagine how it managed to keep going. Rumour said some Brit had paid twenty-five dollars for it a year ago. He'd bought it from a farm boy over near Mortlach.

"I say, is that your dog?" asked the driver, a short, dark-haired young man, not much older than Jack. "Is he a pure-bred border collie?"

Jack shook his head. "No, his father's a border collie, but his mother had lab and terrier in her."

"Is he for sale?" a blond fellow with flashing blue eyes asked.

"Are you daft, Basil?" said the driver. "We can't keep a pup."

"Why not?" Basil came over to Buddy. "He could be the mascot of this blighted bunch of blokes. I'm Basil, by the way." Basil was like a walking advertisement for a handsome British flyer – blond, fit and smartly dressed.

"He's *my* dog," said Jack, standing up beside Buddy.

"Be a good chappie and let us borrow him for a bit." Basil was tickling Buddy under the chin. "We're only here for a couple of months."

The two other fellows joined in. "I could build him a doghouse behind our H-hut," said one of them. "He's more friendly than the sergeant, by crikey," added the other. "More handsome too."

"Basil, you can't just walk off with the fellow's dog," said the driver. "Much as I miss my own." He turned to Jack, "My fox terrier, Max, was killed in the Blitz in '41. Didn't like going to the shelter in the back garden. Stayed in the hall closet under the coats." Jack realized the house must have been bombed.

Jack found himself liking the driver. The others seemed a bit snooty, full of their own importance. He'd noticed that some British flyers acted like everyone in Canada was a hick, or a "colonial," as one pilot had called him. He hoped this batch wouldn't be like that.

The driver shook Jack's hand. "I'm Trevor Knight, of London, England, and these nincompoops are Basil, Dexter and Cheese, otherwise known as Charles." Dexter was pudgy and awkward with a big nose and big feet. Cheese had skin blemishes dotting his face and forehead like small craters on the moon. He had big teeth and a bigger mouth than anyone Jack knew in town. When he grinned it looked like the corners of his mouth ran up to his ears.

Jack listened as the four LACs chatted about home and families and flying planes. Jack warmed to them all finally. Maybe the boys weren't snobs as much as unsure of the ways of Canadian boys. Buddy, meanwhile, had been passed around like a coveted prize and enjoyed the attention.

"Is there any way we could convince you, Jackie boy, to lend us your dog, Mr. Buddy, for the duration of our stay here in this unbelievably empty desert?" asked Basil. He was lanky like Wes McLeod, but really fair, with a small blond moustache, what Ivy Waters would call a cookie duster.

Jack studied the four young flyers. His mind flashed to Sandy, lost somewhere in France. He hoped someone in a French village was helping him.

These guys were a long way from home. Jack remembered studying geography when he was in elementary school, colouring maps and making fancy tags that named the crops, creatures and outstanding features. All of Great Britain had been very green, lush and rainy. Not like Cairn at all. No wonder they were so shocked, probably homesick too. His mind did a fast trip down a dark street – some of them would die in this war, or maybe even in an accident right here in southern Saskatchewan.

Trevor was holding Buddy and crooning to him.

What was Jack going to do?

"I'll think about it," was all he could say.

CHAPTER 9

Wes was sitting on his front stoop eating a brown sugar sandwich when Jack pulled into the lane by the manse. Dr. McLeod was trimming rose bushes beside the stucco bungalow.

"What have you got there?" hollered Wes.

Jack leaned his bike against a barrel of brilliant red geraniums, grabbed Buddy and joined Wes on the steps. "Look what I found!"

McLeod's tortoiseshell Persian, named Gracie Fields after a famous English singer, arched her back, spat and leapt from the wooden rocker on the porch, darting toward the street.

"Gracie Fields doesn't approve of dogs." Wesley reached over and patted the wiggly pup. "Where'd you find him?"

Wes's mother stood behind the screen door in her

apron. "I want to hear too," she said. "Wait a minute and I'll bring lemonade."

She turned and disappeared down the hall. The smell of fresh lemon squares wafted in the air. Wes's mom was younger than Jack's. She took a real interest in whatever the boys were doing.

"What's young Waters brought over?" Dr. McLeod came around the side of the house, wiping his bony hands on a shabby old cardigan. He bent down and scratched Buddy on the chest. "Looks like the Boyles' litter."

"I found this pup on my way to work this morning. I want to keep him. Mom doesn't."

"Don't get your hopes up, Jackie," sighed Dr. McLeod, as his wife appeared with the lemonade. Soon the McLeods were seated on the porch sipping lemonade and listening to Jack's story.

"I know why she said no," Mary McLeod said. "Ivy's not a dog person and she's just had a terrible shock."

"That's what Dad says," Jack agreed.

"I worry about Jimmy and Pete, I do." Dr. McLeod shook his head sadly. "No one sets them much of an example, especially since Mrs. Boyle died of cancer."

"There's a violent streak in old Jerry Boyle," said his wife. "I expect he beats his kids."

"And then there's the drink," Dr. McLeod said. "He and

Pete Nelson like to tie one on most weekends from what I hear."

"Isn't there something we can do?" asked Wes. He had Buddy on his lap and was feeding him crumbs from his square.

"I don't think there's much we can do about the Nelsons or the Boyles. Old Mrs. Nelson comes to church when her arthritis isn't too bad. The Boyles go to the bootlegger instead. But I worry about the guns. You say the mother dog had been shot?"

Jack nodded. "Mrs. Nelson said something about Boyle's old bitch being lame. They probably killed the pups because it was too much trouble to look after them."

"Well, Jackie, my lad, what are you going to do with that beautiful wee dog?" asked Dr. McLeod. He turned and studied his wife Mary's face. "I don't suppose…"

"Gracie Fields would never allow a dog around the place." Mrs. McLeod threw a catnip mouse in the direction of the old cat.

"My wife is a cat person," sighed Dr. McLeod wistfully.

"I'm hoping Dad can talk Mom around."

"Probably not with Sandy missing," said Dr. McLeod. "You know, if I was a younger man, I'd go as a chaplain."

"I'm glad you're too old!" Mary McLeod started clearing the table, loading the plates and glasses onto the tray with a little more vigour than necessary. "Some men have to stay home and hold the fort."

Dr. McLeod kissed the top of his wife's head and escaped to the garden. "I'd best attend to my roses, lads. Good luck finding a home for the wee dog, Jackie."

"Thanks." Jack smiled at Wes. Every time Dr. McLeod got into trouble with his wife he spoke with a thicker Scottish accent.

"Aye," Wes winked at Jack. He knew his father better than Jack did.

"Tell your mom I'm bringing her an apple pie," said Mary McLeod.

"Let's go to your dad's store," suggested Wes. "Maybe your mom's changed her mind."

Jack's mother was polishing the counters. The store smelt of Old Dutch cleanser and Hawes furniture polish. Jack's dad sat on the porch reading the newspaper. Bill Waters loved the puzzles and the comic strip characters – Mutt and Jeff, Li'l Abner and Dagwood. He and the Hobbs twins often sat on the porch of the store and read things out to each other – first the news, then the comics, finally the sports.

Everyone in town liked Jack's dad, Bill, even if he wasn't the best businessman in the world. He'd rather visit and talk than stock a wide variety of groceries. Sometimes he'd forget to reorder until Ivy reminded him. That's why more people went to Cairn General Store for their main supplies. Jack's mom worried all the time about making ends meet, paying the wholesaler, collecting from the people who bought on credit. The way Bill ran the store – or didn't run it – as Ivy said, was a bone of contention between his parents.

Jack glanced between his mom and dad. The tension in the air was as thick as a winter blanket. It looked as if his mother was going to clean and reorganize the whole place. She turned from her work. He could see she was making a real effort not to cry.

"Did you work hard, Jack?"

He nodded.

She continued moving tins of peas and carrots and dusting shelves. "I left you a sandwich wrapped in waxed paper in the icebox at home and there's cold milk to drink. Don't forget to wash your hands thoroughly after handling that dog."

"Hi, Mrs. Waters," said Wes. "Mom's bringing over a pie for your supper. She and Dad are looking forward to your weekly bridge game Monday night."

"Yes, thank you, Wesley."

Jack and Wes walked out into the porch where Buddy had fallen asleep. "I really wanted to keep him," Jack said to Wes. "I feel responsible for him."

"Buddy can sleep in the storeroom for the night," his dad called after him. He followed the boys onto the porch. "Maybe someone at church will want a dog. He'd make a good farm dog."

"I don't want him being a farm dog. I'd never see him." Jack paced up and down the porch. "Are you sure…?"

"No sense pushing, Jack," said his father. "Your mother's really worried about Flo. Hearing about Sandy was bad enough, but if something happened to Flo…"

"Flo's okay." Jack had to defend his sister even if she was miles away.

"Flo's already too feisty for your mother. Running off after her boyfriend to the other side of the world. Working where there are bombs and air raids. Risking life and limb."

Jack nodded. He remembered all too clearly how upset Ivy had been when Flo said she was leaving.

He had vowed then and there to try to be good, or what his mother thought was good. He hated all that tension in the air. It made him feel dizzy.

The two boys sat on the porch. Buddy woke suddenly, shook himself and tumbled toward Jack. He licked Jack's fingers and bounced around. The two boys took the dog for a walk down the street to the train station past the other general store and the Chinese restaurant, where the Hobbs Boys waved through the front window.

A freight train chugged down the track heading toward Swift Current and on to Calgary and points west. The whistle on the steam locomotive blew loudly. Buddy yanked the leash out of Jack's hand and took off down the street as if the devil were chasing him. The boys lit out after him just as the Boyles' Transport truck turned onto the main street. The pup swerved left, the truck swerved right. Buddy rolled under the box, filled with junk lumber and lead pipe. The truck horn jammed and old Boyle leapt down from the cab.

Jack threw himself down on the gravel road and searched under the truck. Wes ran around the other side of the pickup.

"I told Jimmy to get rid of the bitch and those pups. I'm sick and tired of dogs." Boyle swore a blue streak. "Wait till I get my hands on that kid. Needs a belt or two. So do you."

The burly, red-faced man stormed over to where Jack was stretched on the ground. "Aren't you Jackie Waters?" He bent down, his thick body smelling of old sweat and beer, his eyes bleary and his grimy fist clenched. Jack rolled away.

"Here's Buddy," called Wes. "He rolled right under the truck and out the other side."

Jack leapt to his feet and took off with Wes and Buddy, leaving Old Boyle shouting at the air. Three women had come out of the restaurant and stood watching, their arms folded across their chests. The Hobbs Boys stepped onto the pavement and headed in Boyle's direction.

"Hang on a moment, Jerry," said Melvin as he strode toward old Boyle.

"Leave the kid alone." Arnie Hobbs spoke with more authority than Jack had ever heard from any one of the Hobbses. "We don't want any trouble here in Cairn."

Old Boyle shook slightly as he stood up and dusted off his trousers. He could see everyone on the main street glaring at him.

"How about you and Arnie and I have a cup of coffee," Mel said.

"We'll leave Jimmy's dad in good hands," said Wes. "At least Buddy's all right."

"I'm taking him back to the store and tying him up. He's had enough brushes with death for a whole lifetime." Jack hugged the pup to his chest.

"You could have been killed, you dumb little mutt," Jack said.

Wes patted Buddy's head. "How're you going to handle this, Jack?"

"I don't know."

All Jack knew for sure was that the dog was a gift. Maybe a gift he couldn't keep, but still, a gift.

CHAPTER 10

Sunday morning the congregation stood as Ivy played the introduction to the hymn on the wheezy organ. The choir wore their black gowns, the women sporting shiny white collars and the men with their white shirts and dark neckties showing. Jack stood with the tenors and Wes towered in the middle of the bass baritones.

There was a commotion at the back of the church. Jack looked up to see Trevor, Basil and their buddies Cheese and Dexter tiptoe in and slip into the back pew.

Most of the congregation turned to glare at the latecomers and then smiled a welcome. It was always a treat having the "boys from away" as the young flyers were called. And it was a long walk into the village, easy enough for them to misjudge the time.

The singing began with great gusto. Ivy liked a strong attack on the first line, but even she was taken aback by the powerful voices coming from the back pew.

Trevor and Basil sang lustily and by the second verse they'd moved to harmony. By the close of the hymn the whole congregation and the choir looked ready to applaud. None of the other flyers had ever been great singers, in fact none of them could carry a tune in a basket.

Dr. McLeod gave the opening prayer and announced the next hymn. Jack found it and looked up. Trevor was grinning at him and waving his hand out in the aisle. Jack tried not to laugh.

The sopranos were whispering among themselves. "Can we talk them into joining the choir, do you think?"

"Maybe if we had a couple of young girls."

Ivy frowned and the sopranos stopped talking.

During the sermon Jack's mind wandered. He'd left Buddy in the back room of the store with a wall of packing cases keeping him out of the store proper. Jack's mother hadn't let him sleep in the store with the dog for fear of hoboes or burglars.

When Jack had gotten up he'd raced to release the poor pup, who was so glad to see him he piddled. It warmed Jack's heart to have anyone that glad to see him even though it dampened the floor and he had to mop up.

He'd taken Buddy for a walk and a romp on the baseball diamond. He'd tried talking to his mother at breakfast about keeping the dog, but she was too distracted. "I'm sorry, Jack, I can't deal with this now. The church pays me an honorarium for playing the organ. They deserve good service."

She had moved on to her usual Sunday instructions. "Polish your shoes. Slick your hair down. Make sure your dad remembers his tie." Then she'd left for church.

Maybe, after all, he should let Trevor and the other boys take Buddy. In a few months he might figure out a way to keep him himself.

"Let us pray," Dr. McLeod interrupted Jack's reverie. The long prayer covered the king, the queen, the princesses, the prime minister, the armed forces, the sick, the injured, the dying. Jack sighed and thought of Sandy.

Arnie Hobbs nudged him. "Pay attention, Jackie, we're singing the last hymn."

After the last chord, Jack ran down the back stairs, dumped his robe on a hanger and raced up the basement steps to greet Trevor and Basil. His mother was already holding Trevor's elbow as Basil looked on.

"Guess who's joining the choir," she said happily. "And Basil and Trevor are coming for dinner. The other boys,

Dexter and, if I got it right, Cheese, are joining the McLeods."

"I need my tea," said Basil. "I missed it, walking to church."

"Where's Buddy?" asked Trevor.

"In the back room of the store," said Bill. "Come along, and we'll let the dog out into the summer air."

"Have you decided yet?" asked Trevor.

"What?" asked Jack.

He knew what Trevor wanted but he needed to take his time. Buddy's whole future depended on this decision.

"I'll keep working on your mom, Jackie, but for now anyway these fellows seem to want Buddy." Bill led the way to the back of the store and opened the door. The smell of disinfectant soap, candies and pickles wafted out as Buddy tumbled down the steps like a rubber ball with dancing legs and wagging tail. Jack and Trevor knelt to stop his escape.

Watching Trevor tussle with Buddy, Jack felt his resolve turn to melted butter. The smile on Trevor's face as he played with Buddy, the croon in his voice, made up his mind.

"I couldn't find a home for the dog. You can take him." Then Jack added. "But I have to have visiting privileges."

"That's wizard," said Trevor. He picked Buddy up and carried him a few steps before the wiggling mass leapt out of his arms and led them a merry chase. A flock of sparrows lifted off from the caraganas as they came down the street to the house.

The rich smells of baked ham and scalloped potatoes reached Jack and the student pilots as they turned into the back lane. The boys arranged a rope and a stake in the ground. Bill filled a bowl with fresh water from the cistern.

Ivy stood behind the screen door. "Make sure he's tied up securely. I don't want him getting into the raspberry bushes."

Everyone trooped into the house, wiping the dust from their feet on the sisal mat. The table was set for Sunday dinner with the Blue Willow china plates and cups. Besides the ham and potatoes that had been cooking while church was going on, there was tomato juice, green relish, bread and butter pickles, sliced white bread and butter and creamed corn. Dad asked grace and everyone passed their plates. Jack snuck a small heel of the ham into his pocket for the pup whining pitifully in the backyard.

"So tell me where you received your musical training, boys," asked Mom. "Do you play instruments as well as sing?"

CHAPTER 11

It turned out that Basil had gone to a choir school and sung in a fancy cathedral boy's choir. When he spoke, it was like listening to the BBC announcer on the radio news from England.

Trevor had come from a large musical family in a crowded London neighbourhood. He had an uncle who danced and sang in musical revues. Trevor had actually met George Formby, the famous comic singer, and Gracie Fields, the glamorous British performer, when he'd visited his uncle backstage at the Pantages Theatre.

"Unfortunately, both my dad and my uncle like the booze too much. That's why I drink just tea and soft drinks." So saying, Trevor poured himself another glass of ginger ale.

"Couldn't you have gotten a job entertaining the troops?" asked Jack.

Trevor's face clouded. "I wanted out, especially after our house was bombed and our dog died." He sighed as if there was a much bigger story he wasn't ready to share.

"Why'd you join the air force?"

"Someone has to protect our country," Trevor said. "Everyone in our senior class joined up."

"You have no idea how bad it is," said Basil. "The fear grinds you down. Democracy could disappear. I don't fancy giving the Nazi salute to anyone."

The conversation around the table died. Basil held his fork before him like a conductor's baton. "I don't want to sound like a recruitment poster – but if you went through one bombing raid, watched airplanes being shot down or listened to one broadcast of Nazi propaganda –"

"Let alone losing your home and your dog," Trevor interrupted.

Jack nodded. These young men knew what they thought and weren't afraid to say it. It was one thing to read about the war or watch the news at the movie theatre, but it was another to decide what you thought about it. Basil and Trevor had really thought about it. Jack's world seemed suddenly bigger.

Ivy frowned. She carried a pile of plates into the kitchen and left them for Dad to wash. Dad always did the Sunday dinner dishes.

Jack could see that this discussion bothered her. He glanced up at his dad. His dad nodded.

"Why don't we adjourn to the parlour? Have a little music." Dad shooed everyone into the living room.

Mom opened the piano and hesitated. "Who wants to play? Jackie plays, but he never practices and I just finished playing at church."

Trevor sat on the piano stool, lifted his feet off the floor, and twirled around once. He played a few chords. "Nice tone." He ran his surprisingly long fingers over the keys in a lively popular song.

"I keep it tuned," said Ivy. "I can't stand any song going off-key." As Trevor played, Ivy's worried face relaxed. She looked younger than she had for ages. She loved music so much and here were musicians in her own living room in Cairn.

"I know what you mean," said Trevor. "My uncle let me use his piano when he was on the road. He kept his in tune himself."

"This was my first husband Jack's piano," Ivy said, sorting through a pile of music that had been undisturbed on a shelf near the piano. "He wouldn't play after he came home from the Great War. He said there was nothing to sing about. The piano gathered dust for months. I got it tuned after he died and played it myself."

A hundred questions crowded into Jack's head. Just how long was his uncle home before he died? Had he died of war wounds or the 1918 influenza epidemic? Where was Jack's dad while this was going on?

All he knew for sure was that Uncle Jack Waters died after the First World War. Florence, Jack's half-sister, never saw her dad. If Uncle Jack had died of influenza, wouldn't he have been told about it? Flo seemed to know. Jack remembered Flo's promise to tell him more. She couldn't do it now.

Trevor and Basil were singing "You are my Sunshine." Trevor's voice was a bell-like tenor, the notes pure and crisp as fresh snow. Jack's mind and body were pulled into the music and he let the niggling questions about what had happened years ago fade. He felt something akin to flying as the notes blended and filled the room with melody.

His mother handed out some Gilbert and Sullivan and Cole Porter sheet music. The small house filled with the sound of really good voices.

"Wes would love this." Jack couldn't keep the excitement out of his voice. "He's a bass too, Basil."

"Why don't you go get him?" asked Basil.

"He doesn't do much on Sundays, being a PK and all." Jack chuckled.

"What's a PK?" asked Trevor. "Some kind of weird religion?"

"Hardly," laughed Ivy Waters.

"A PK is a preacher's kid," Jack said.

Trevor shook his head. "So much to learn and so little time."

"Maybe we should form a quartet," suggested Basil. "It would keep our minds off the war. We've already got a band formed at the base. I've got a few musical ideas I'd like to try out and Trevor is a fine musician. Maybe we could write and perform together. How's that for an idea?" Basil certainly liked to talk.

Trevor, playing a medley of old ballads and Scottish tunes, smiled but didn't answer. He had a light touch – his playing seemingly effortless.

"I've got a brilliant idea!" Basil bounced up out of his chair. "Why don't we put on a musical evening – a musical revue?"

"Great idea." Trevor struck a series of chords. "There's lots of talent on the base. We've got students, ground crew and instructors to choose from."

"There's quite a bit of talent in the village too," chimed in Ivy. "The Hobbs family are all singers."

"There's the fiddlers in Mortlach," said Jack. "And Dad likes telling jokes."

"I heard that." Dad stuck his head in from the kitchen. "Someone told me the Boyles step dance."

"I didn't know that," said Jack, trying to imagine the red-faced elder Boyle doing anything that pleasant.

"When I first came to town we used to have lots of musical evenings," Ivy said with a sigh. "Jack organized them. That's how we met, Jack and I. I came to town with the Chautauqua. I was a Chautauqua girl."

"What's that?" asked Basil. "Sounds like some woolly beast."

"It was a summer event with music, lectures and all kinds of entertainment," said Jack's mom. "It travelled from place to place, all across the Midwest in both Canada and the United States. There were local participants and touring artists."

"And what did a Chautauqua girl do?" asked Basil.

Ivy's face seemed to lose years as she spoke. "I sang solos and I also accompanied other singers on the piano."

"Do they still have them?" asked Trevor.

Ivy shook her head. "For some reason they died out. Anyway, when Jack died I lost track of it. I had my baby, Florence, to take care of."

"Well," said Basil. "I think it's time good old Cairn had another celebration."

Jack watched his mother sitting in her armchair, not quite sure what her response should be to the handsome, talented pair of flyers in her usually quiet parlour.

"When's your next holiday?" asked Basil. "Could we pull together a fête?"

Jack looked puzzled. "What's a fête?"

"A fête is like a community party," Mom said, and added, "Dominion Day's coming, but that's too soon, we'll need several weeks of practice."

"That's right," said Basil. "Ground school and flying lessons will keep us pretty busy the next couple of months. We won't have a lot of free time."

"Too bad my older brother isn't here. He plays a great cornet," Trevor added.

"Is he in the forces?" asked Jack.

"No, Terry's at home. He's…" Trevor bit his lip.

"What about Labour Day? That's the first weekend in September," Ivy said, cutting Trevor off.

The young airman bowed his head and picked a couple of crumbs off his uniform. Jack wondered if he was missing his family. Jack couldn't imagine being thousands of miles away from his. It was bad enough having his sister gone all the time, not even coming home from Moose Jaw on weekends like she used to.

"What do you think, Jack?" Basil asked. "That's just before we graduate – if we don't wash out."

"We head back to school the Tuesday following Labour Day. We'd have lots of time till then."

"Labour Day, then," said Trevor.

"Smashing!" said Basil. "That gives us plenty of time to put out a call for acts, line up the program and rehearse."

Crash! Clatter! Clump! Noises and cries of pain came from the kitchen.

Jack ran. His father lay sprawled on the floor, a splintered stool beside him and the Blue Willow meat platter resting on his heaving chest.

"Are you all right?" Ivy cried.

"It only hurts when I laugh," smiled Bill through his teeth. "I saved the platter. On the other hand, my back doesn't feel so great."

Ivy rushed to the telephone, lifted the crank. "Should I call the doctor?"

"If you do, everyone on the line will know I'm out of commission."

"How?" asked Trevor.

"It's a party line. There's fourteen people could listen in. Besides, the operator has a mouth as big as the Grand Canyon." Bill tried to grin.

Jack bent and rescued the platter, hoping his father wasn't too badly hurt. He'd made a joke of it, but then he always did that. Jack and Trevor and Basil helped Bill up and half carried, half steered him into the living room where he collapsed on the couch.

Bill complained and moaned all the way.

"I'll cycle over to the doctor's house," said Jack.

"I'll be all right," his father protested weakly.

"I'd rather have him check you out," said Ivy.

"We'll get Buddy and head back to the base," said Trevor. "Thanks for a wonderful meal, Mrs. Waters. I haven't had a joint for tea since I don't know how long. Not with all the rationing back home."

"We have rationing," said Jack. "But I guess it's nothing compared to yours."

"The Cairn Cosmopolitan Music Society has just had its founding meeting," Basil said. "I can hear those voices soaring already. Thanks for tea."

Jack shook his head. Since when was a ham a joint, and Sunday dinner a tea? He liked Trevor a lot, but Basil was too much. He was a one-man band, his enthusiasm as boundless as Buddy's.

Jack walked with them into the backyard, the two flyers bouncing with energy, talking about how to look after Buddy, how to get practice time for their music. Buddy leaped and yipped as Jack untied the rope, then hurled his little body at the flyers as soon as he was released.

Jack bent down and tousled Buddy's thick black fur behind his ears. "You be a good dog, you hear me? Don't chase cars or planes and don't bite." He buried his face in the dog's furry ruff, smelling that clean puppy smell and a trace of dust and sweat. He handed the dog to Basil.

"Are you coming out to work tomorrow after school?" asked Trevor.

"We're in the first H-hut." Basil grasped Buddy's leash and Trevor picked up the bag with the dish, an old towel for company and some food in a paper sack.

"Cheese is going to build Buddy a wee house," Basil continued, "and Dexter will walk him. Life is looking up, one might even say soaring. We'll have a swell time staging this fête. The sky is not the limit for any of us. Right, Jackie?"

Jack nodded. He grabbed his bike and walked partway down the main street with the two young flyers before he had to turn off. As he pedalled up the hill toward the doctor's house, he turned and watched the group leave. Buddy trotted along on his leash between Basil and Trevor, out past the train station toward the air base.

A sudden gust of chilly wind chased tumbleweeds down the gravel street beside the house.

Buddy looked so small, struggling to keep up with the long legs and the steady walk of the two young men. Jack was tempted to run after them and take the dog back. He had saved Buddy. Why couldn't he keep him?

Life wasn't as simple as he'd always thought it was. Before the flying school, before the flyers, before Buddy.

CHAPTER 12

Jack needed time to think about the day's events, the energy that had been let loose like a miniature volcano in the church and in his house. He'd never seen his mother so excited.

He took a deep breath and shook himself like a damp dog. Then he rode over to the doctor's house. The doctor was out in the country delivering a baby but his wife said she'd tell him about Jack's dad's accident. "Sounds like something Bill would do." She smiled.

A village was like a big family. The good, the bad, the strange and the run-of-the-mill – they all lived in Cairn. Until the aerodrome came, it had been Jack's whole, private world. Now it seemed his village had shrunk to a dot on a prairie that stretched for thousands of miles, all the way to a hospital in England and, he hoped, somewhere safe in the French countryside.

The streets of Cairn lay quiet in the Sunday afternoon sun. Pine siskins serenaded from the elms. Most of the adult males of the town were snoozing on old couches in kitchens, or, if they were lucky, on a porch swing or hammock. Mothers and older sisters tidied dishes and gossiped. Children played quietly in yards. All the stores were closed and shuttered. Even the Chinese restaurant closed on Sundays until suppertime.

Jack hoped Buddy would be all right. There was only a week more of school and then Jack would be working five days a week at the air base, able to see Buddy every day. This next week would be pretty easy. There were a couple of exams left and the field day with the kids from Mortlach.

Jack pulled up behind his house and parked his bike. He went in, letting the screen door bang behind him. He'd have to fix that. His dad was always trying to get around to it. Jack could hear his voice coming from the parlour.

"Maybe that's the doctor."

"What are we going to do if you're laid up, Bill?" His mother's voice sounded anxious.

"We'll have to wait and see what Doctor Kowalski says. Right now it just hurts like heck and my left leg feels numb."

"The doctor's out on call." Jack poured himself a glass of

cold water from the pitcher in the icebox and joined his parents. "He'll come when he gets back. How are you?"

"Oh, I'll live."

"If you had fixed that stool when I asked you to…" Jack's mom knitted furiously on a khaki scarf for a soldier. "And we had such a great afternoon too."

"Do you need anything, Dad?" Jack was itching to wander over to Wes's house and tell him about Trevor and Basil's plans. "Something to read?"

"I'm too sore. It's a sorry Sunday when I can't read the *Reader's Digest* and get my supply of jokes for the week. Who wants stale jokes? That's worse than stale bread."

"This is serious, Bill," Ivy chided. "Why do you have to make everything into a joke?"

"I thought you married me because I made you laugh."

Bill Waters winked at Jack. He tried to shift on the pillows and grimaced. "Did you hear the one about the man with the wooden leg named Charlie?"

"What was the name of his good leg?" asked Jack. It was an old joke. One he and his dad used every once in a while. "I'm going over to Wes's to tell him about the big Labour Day concert. Is there anything you need before I go?"

"Find out when Catherine Anne is coming home. I need her in the choir, especially now that we've got big plans." His mother sounded downright happy.

"You need Cathy to keep those young flyboys happy," laughed Bill. "Who's going to warn the poor girl she's being used as bait?"

"Bill!"

Jack hurried out before anything more could be said.

The McLeods were sitting in the side yard. Lemonade, tea and cookies sat on the wooden table. Wes was reading Shakespeare's *Macbeth* to bone up for the exam. He'd ace it anyway. English was his best subject.

His mother and father were chatting. Jack interrupted.

"I've got news. Some good and some bad. Dad fell and hurt his back – and Trevor and Basil are going to sing in the choir and help us put on a concert for Labour Day."

"Is Bill all right?" asked Dr. McLeod. "Should I go over to your house?"

"It's his bones that need fixing, not his soul, Ian." The minister's wife laughed. "You just want to go talk to Bill, admit it."

Jack grabbed a couple of cookies, threw himself into a folding chair, and described the afternoon's adventures. Then he remembered Ivy's request. "Mom wants to know when Cathy's coming home. She needs another strong alto."

"Oho, do I sense a little conspiracy?" asked Mrs. McLeod. "Just how old are Trevor and Basil?"

"Well, they've got to be over eighteen to be in the RAF," said Jack.

"Cathy's been so busy at Normal School learning how to be a teacher that I don't think she's had time for a boyfriend," said Wes.

"She'll have plenty of time for that nonsense when she's older," said Dr. McLeod. "She's taking the summer off and then she's been hired to teach elementary school right here in Cairn."

"When's she coming home?" asked Jack.

"She'll be on the train tonight." Mrs. McLeod gathered up the tea things and carried them inside.

"I'll pop over and see how Bill is," said Dr. McLeod.

"We'll go for a walk and check out the poison ivy crop," said Wes.

"Don't you go sneaking any baseball mitts with you," his father said. "Think what the church elders would say."

As the boys strolled down the street Jack said, "If it weren't for the church elders, I bet he'd let you play games on a Sunday afternoon."

"Dad doesn't think God is as fussy as old farmers. Neither do I. Jesus wasn't much for following the rules and regulations of his day."

"I guess you're right," Jack said. "I let Trevor and Basil take Buddy to the base."

"As a mascot? That sounds like a good idea."

"I didn't have a chance to talk it over with you. Do you think I did the right thing?"

"Tell me more about Trevor and Basil."

"They are great!" Jack said. "As I said they're going to join the choir and they want to write a musical revue for Labour Day weekend."

"Then chances are Buddy's in good hands, Jackie."

The boys strolled through town, hands in their pockets, kicking pebbles ahead of them. Jimmy Boyle, home from Moose Jaw, drove past them in his dad's beat-up pickup truck. He shook his fist at Jack, raced his motor and sped out of town.

"What a jerk!"

"Dad says the Boyles step dance. Who would have guessed?"

Wes shook his head. "I, for one, can't see them doing it. Jimmy doesn't look like a dancer. More like a boxer. What's he mad at you for?"

"His dad probably got after him," replied Jack. "I think he's mad because I rescued Buddy and because I got a 'cushy' job at the airfield."

"You work hard, Jack."

"Jimmy doesn't know that."

The two friends walked to the tiny park at the end of the block. Jack flopped down on an old swing.

"Trevor looks awfully young to be a pilot." Wes hung upside down from the frame of a baby swing that was long gone, then somersaulted to the ground.

"Dad said a lot of the English boys lie about their age to get in the air force. Maybe Trevor did. He doesn't need to shave yet. I could tell looking at him."

Wes laughed. "If he did, he's not the only one around here that hasn't told the whole truth. You've got a few secrets of your own."

"If you ever tell, I'll –"

"I know. It's a secret I have to take to the grave with me. How Jack Waters learned to fly."

"Don't push me, Wes."

"I cross my heart and hope to die. Okay?"

"Wes," his mother called from the McLeods' front porch. "Time to go. Dad is taking us to the Ambassador Café in Moose Jaw before we fetch Cathy."

Wes hurried away, leaving Jack swinging lazily. He thought about Basil and Trevor. They were starting training and had no idea that he was ahead of them in flying skills. He jumped off the swing and headed out of the sleepy village, instead of home to check on his dad. Sometimes his secret clamoured to get out like a drowning gopher out of a hole.

J ack wandered out the gravel road that led to the Hobbs' farm with its wonderful swimming hole. Melvin and Arnie had dammed the creek, decades ago, before they went to the Great War. He couldn't walk that far today. He just wanted to put some distance between himself and his life in Cairn.

In the last few years so many people had passed through his life, like the trains rolling across the prairies or the ducks and geese that spent summers on the sloughs and ponds around Thunder Creek. Everyone was bound for somewhere else – off to the war in Europe or the Far East, or moving to Calgary, Edmonton, Regina or Saskatoon, where they would work in munitions factories or manufacturing plants.

Now these two young guys had walked into his life and stirred things up. He wanted to join in and get involved but he worried about investing too much in people who were just going to up and leave in a couple of months.

Jack shaded his eyes from the setting sun and scanned the sky. A flock of geese flying in formation headed west to the wetlands near Thunder Creek. He whistled a crazy song his mom had taught him to play: "Mares eat oats and does eat oats and little lambs eat ivy."

His mother hadn't played funny songs since Sandy went missing. She'd had days when she hardly talked because she was so sad. Every couple of weeks she'd pack a box of tinned goods and treats to send to Flo. The last time she had put in a bag of liquorice allsorts, Flo's favourites. "It's the only sweet things she's likely to get," she'd said.

She'd taped the box carefully, trying to guarantee its safe delivery to somewhere in England. "All we can do is hope she doesn't get sent to a field hospital near the front lines. That's really dangerous."

Jack figured if Flo had the chance to go to the front, she would. She couldn't tell them straight out. The censors wouldn't let her. Besides if she told, Mom would worry all the more.

Mom once said that if Jack had been through the First World War, the Depression, the dirty thirties with the dust and drought, and now Hitler, he'd know why she was a worrywart.

After Flo left for England, Ivy had confided in Jack, "You're all I've got left, Jackie. Whatever you do, don't get hurt."

He'd promised not to. But if someone needed help, what would he do?

CHAPTER 13

After winning the five-hundred-yard race at the field day on Monday, Jack was feeling pretty chipper. Wes had won the broad jump. On Tuesday, Jack and Wes wrote their last exams. Jack knew he'd aced Science and Math. He was a winner whether anyone knew it or not.

In the afternoon Wes's sister Cathy came to the high school to talk about careers. She sounded a little nervous and flustered, probably because her little brother Wes was sitting there, grinning like a gawky crane with red hair and freckles.

Wes figured Cathy was really there because the principal wanted her to meet the other teachers and get a feel for the way the school worked, since she would be teaching Grades One to Four in September.

Jack was so amazed at how pretty Cathy looked in her pastel blue skirt and white blouse, her blondish hair cut in a short bob, her blue eyes dancing, that he couldn't hear much of what she was saying. He'd always thought of Cathy as Wes's skinny older sister. When had she turned into a beautiful young woman, he wondered? Too bad she was nearly nineteen.

Girls. Jack smiled. Maybe he was the one who had changed.

After school, Wes, Jack and Cathy strolled down the street to the Chinese restaurant for milkshakes. "Is the principal always so formal?" Cathy asked. "He didn't seem so serious when he interviewed me at Easter."

"When he's in front of the whole school, Mr. Mackintosh tries to sound severe," said Wes. "But during the World Series playoffs he hauls his short-wave radio into class so we can keep up with the score."

"That's right!" Jack had a hard time speaking around the knot in his throat. He felt as if his feet and hands had lead weights in them. He'd never felt this way around Cathy before, not even last Christmas when she was home for the holidays. "He made jokes when he was handing me the prize for winning the race against Mortlach's finest." Jack blushed. There, at least Cathy would know he had some skills. He wished he could tell her he could fly.

"Jack's our best runner, for sure." Wes gazed at Jack. "Not as modest as I thought, though."

A couple of grade twelve students in the front booth waved to Cathy. "We heard you guys are planning a big musical night," said Tommy Thompson, the pharmacist's son. "Too bad we'll miss it."

"No loss, though," said Earl, a skinny guy with bushy black eyebrows that met in the middle. "We're not very talented."

"Why are you going to miss it?" Cathy asked.

"We're going to join the Royal Canadian Air Force," said Tommy. "We're off to the manning depot in Regina to sign up."

"Will you be training at the Moose Jaw base?" Jack asked.

"Don't know yet," Tommy said. "Probably."

"Maybe you'll be able to make the fête, then," Cathie said.

"I hear you have two hotshot RAF flyers helping." Earl drained his chocolate soda with a noisy slurp.

"They haven't flown anything yet," Wes said. "They just got here. But they can sure sing."

"Unlike us," said Earl. "Say, did you hear Jimmy Boyle and Repete tried to sign up? They lied about their age."

"Nobody believed them." Tommy laughed. "My cousin in Moose Jaw told me. He saw them on the street. They worked in construction for a few days but got fired for being late. So they're back in the village, swearing and fighting as usual."

"Dad heard that Jimmy's driving for his dad," Jack said. "I don't know what Repete's doing."

"Jimmy's mad at Jack for rescuing one of his puppies," said Wes.

"Watch out for him," said Tommy. "He holds grudges a long time. Shot holes in my dad's sign because he wouldn't sell him cigarettes. No proof, though. The Mounties couldn't do anything."

The two grads paid Mr. Wong and headed out the door.

"I have to meet these RAF fellows." Cathy blushed. "Everyone's been telling me about them. I hope they aren't snobs."

"You'll meet them tonight at choir practice," said Jack. "See for yourself."

The three kids carried their milkshakes to a booth by the window, next to the Hobbs twins. Howie Wong, the restaurant owner, hummed as he polished the tables. "Coming In on a Wing and a Prayer" was his favourite tune this week.

"Mr. Wong should sing in the chorus at the fête," suggested Wes.

"I'll tell Basil and Trevor." Jack sipped his chocolate shake and gazed at Cathy McLeod from under his lowered eyelids. Suddenly a voice from the neighbouring booth spoke what Jack was only thinking. "You've turned into quite the young lady, Catherine Anne McLeod." Melvin Hobbs swooped his old fedora off his head and bowed. Arnie touched the brim of his worn straw hat.

"Thanks, Mr. Hobbs." Cathy smiled at them.

"Glad to see you aren't heading off to war, my dear," said Arnie.

Cathy sighed. "I wish there was another way of making tyrants go away."

"We get more proficient at killing each other with each passing decade," Arnie sighed. "I heard the Nazis are working on a new rocket."

"We're learning to kill people hundreds of miles away," said Mel.

"Whatever happened to 'Thou shalt not kill'?" Cathy said. "Educated people should figure out alternatives to fighting."

There was a sudden silence in the restaurant. Most Canadians were behind the war effort one hundred percent. It took a pretty determined person to voice a contrary view. Jack admired Cathy's spunk. She was a pretty strong character. He didn't agree with her, though. Jack didn't know what else they could do now but fight.

Cathy handed Wes a quarter for her milkshake and stood.

"Good luck with your new job!" Melvin lifted his hot coffee as if it was a toast and took a sip. "This stuff gets worse by the week, Howie."

Mr. Wong shrugged. "It's hard to get good beans." He took the money from Wes, rang the cash register and tossed the change into a small rubber tray.

"Sounds like you've got *grounds* for complaining," Jack giggled.

"Don't be a *drip*, Jack." Wes pocketed the change and headed for the door. "We better get *percolating* down the street if we want to get any dinner before choir practice."

"Puns are the lowest form of humour, little brother."

"We can't be serious all the time, Cathy."

"Have you noticed," Arnie spoke loudly as the kids headed for the door, "how kids have to stop eating snacks so they can eat supper? If I did that, I'd weigh a ton."

"As I recall, when you were their age you could eat a horse and have room for dessert," laughed Melvin.

"That was then," Arnie said.

The three young people sauntered down the street. When they rounded the corner, a fierce gust of wind roared in their direction. Dark clouds gathered in the north. Jack lifted the front of his T-shirt to cover his face and keep the dust out of his mouth and eyes. Gravel stung his exposed flesh.

"Will the flyers be able to get to town if this wind keeps up?" asked Cathy.

Wes glanced at his sister. "They have an old jalopy they bought off the last bunch of LACs. Anyway, why are you so interested?"

"Don't you have a boyfriend in Regina?" Jack tried to keep his question casual.

"None of your business, Jackie Waters," said Cathy. "I just wanted to know if we would have a good-sized choir at rehearsal."

"Sure, Cathy." Wes chuckled. "You're just interested in the choir."

"We believe you," added Jack. Suddenly he wasn't sure he wanted Cathy meeting Basil and Trevor.

When they reached Jack's back porch, it had started to rain. Wes and Cathy followed Jack inside. It was so dark he turned the lights on.

"Where's your mom?" Cathy glanced around the unusually quiet house.

"Ever since Dad threw his back out, she's been running the store. He sits on a couch with weights on his left foot – supervising." Jack shrugged. "I'm learning how to cook."

"You'll make some girl a wonderful husband," laughed Wes.

"There's nothing the matter with a man learning to cook." Cathy started putting away the dishes left in the dish drainer by the sink. "Dad cooks. Mind you, I hate it myself.

But I admire men who aren't afraid of doing 'women's work.'" She gave Jack a big smile.

Jack discovered that for some reason his heart was beating fast. He looked at the table and spotted some crumbs from his lunch. He quickly wiped them off the oilcloth with a damp rag and hung the rag over the pump handle by the sink.

Cathy headed into the living room, or the parlour as some people still called it. She sat down at the piano and played "Chopsticks." Wes took the lower octaves and played the second part. Jack turned on the brass banker's lamp that stood on top of the piano, a faint smell of Cathy's lily of the valley cologne tickling his nose.

Wind rattled the window. Spritzes of fine dust sifted through the cracks around the frames and under the door. No one would be flying today.

Suddenly the lights went out. Cathy and Wes paused in their playing for a moment, then laughed and carried on their duet in the darkened room. Jack went to the kitchen and opened the drawer that held the candles and matches. The Waters family were always prepared, Mom made sure of that.

He lit a candle and carried it into the living room and put it on the top of the piano. Wes and Cathy had moved on to more complicated pieces, the tumbling notes fighting against the fury of the storm.

The wind howled around the house. Rain pinged against the window like nails in a galvanized steel bucket. The lights didn't come on.

"That's quite the storm," commented Cathy.

Wes glanced out the window. "Too bad Mom can't hear us practicing. She'd be pleased."

Jack envied them their relaxed attitude. His mother hated lightning. She'd always wake him up when there was a bad storm. He remembered as a small boy sitting in the kitchen sipping hot cocoa, wearing his cowboy pyjamas and wrapped in a Hudson's Bay blanket. If the wind really howled, they went down into the small dirt basement that smelled of mildew and mice.

Dad wouldn't do it. He could sleep through anything and refused to worry about things he couldn't change.

Jack stared at a yellow moth flitting around the candle. It dove, rolled and flew closer and closer to the flame, like a tiny airplane. Jack had never seen a moth so large and colourful. Its wings, like a dew-covered spiderweb, shone with flecks of gold. Jack was transfixed by the orange flame flickering in the gloom and the bright moth in its curious dance. He raised his hand, ready to blow the candle out or pinch the flame, but he was too late.

With a flash of yellow and blue and a soft hiss the delicate body dropped onto the polished wooden surface of the piano.

Jack shivered. He felt as if, as his mother put it, "someone just walked over my grave."

"What if there's a tornado?" asked Jack. "We should go to the basement, just in case."

"Come on, Jack, it's a storm not a catastrophe!" Wes peered out through the glass in the unused front door. "But wait, what do I see on the horizon – it's a tornado and this is Kansas and we'll all be twirled away to Oz."

"Okay, and I'm the Cowardly Lion," sighed Jack. "But I'd feel safer in the basement."

"Sis, let's leave our ungracious host and run for home. Mom will probably serve cookies to us survivors." Wes headed for the back door.

"Are you coming with us?" Cathy asked.

"No, I'll see you later at choir practice." Jack took some carrots out to peel for supper.

"What a cautious fellow you are."

Jack blushed. "Mom and Dad will be home soon. I'm supposed to start supper."

As Cathy stood by the door, tying a scarf around her blond hair, Jack wished he could impress her. But it wasn't going to happen today. In a moment Cathy and Wes were out the door, leaving him in the kitchen working on the carrots.

The storm had passed long before choir practice, thank goodness. Jack and his parents had supper. Then Ivy headed over to the church. Bill headed to the couch with his *Reader's Digest*.

"So tonight the flyers join the choir," said his dad. "Your mother is sure pleased about that."

"And Cathy's back from Normal School," sighed Jack.

"Maybe she'll fall for one of the flyers," Bill laughed. "In spring a young person's fancy turns to love."

"That's what I'm afraid of," whispered Jack so his dad couldn't hear him. "I'm going now," he called out as he headed for the door. "See you later."

Jack sprinted along the gravel street. Up ahead he spotted the jalopy parked in front of the church already. Cathy and Basil were shaking hands and laughing about something. Trevor was climbing out of the driver's seat and Wes stood by the side of the car, hands in his pockets, watching the whole scene. Some friend he was.

Jack kicked a loose pile of tiny stones so hard he stubbed his big toe. He thought back to Cathy and Wes standing in his kitchen earlier, laughing at the storm. He wondered how he looked to them, and suddenly he saw those nights long ago, sitting in the kitchen with his mother, in a new way. He'd always thought she did it to comfort him. Now, he wasn't sure. Who had been comforting whom?

CHAPTER 14

With school over, Jack worked every day at the air base. They'd had no further news of Sandy, but Flo had written several times, talking about the long hours she worked nursing wounded fliers.

She missed Sandy a lot and worried about him but said she had quite a few friends. Some of the other nurses had boyfriends they hadn't heard from. Flo got to go to dances because the nearby bases would send a bus for the nurses to come for the evening. They danced to live bands and orchestras. Sometimes entertainers put on variety shows for the troops. Jack was glad it wasn't all work.

She had hinted that she might be moved. She couldn't say where to or when but she had written a strange sentence or two in her last letter. He didn't think his mother had figured out what Flo was trying to tell them.

"I'm looking forward to taking a hike with friends soon down the winding road leading from this hospital to a much smaller one. Around the bend are fields with farmers clearing crops. It's pretty rustic but the scenery will be different.

"How did school go, Jack? Did you excel in French and English?"

"Flo knows French and English aren't your best subjects," Dad said after reading the letter and passing it on to him. "What's she talking about?"

"She's probably forgotten he's our Math whiz kid," said his mother. "I'm glad she's getting out with friends her own age. Flo is better at this than I would ever be. I worry more than she does."

Dad had leaned across the table and given her a peck on the cheek. "We all do the best we can, Ivy."

After Jack had read the letter twice, he'd decided that Flo was being shipped out to a field hospital somewhere near the front, probably in France. He was proud of her – and a tad worried. Were field hospitals safe?

Jack's own life had settled into a comfortable routine, revolving around his job at the base, the choir and hanging out with Trevor, Basil, Cathy, Cheese and Dexter. Wes had gone off to be a counsellor at a church camp but would be back soon. Jack missed him. Wes could be pretty serious but he was a lot of fun too.

There'd been a couple of minor accidents at the base but nothing really bad. Jack was working hard, cycling out to the airfield every morning at eight-thirty to find Harold and Angus already at work.

One morning in mid-July Jack heard a loud shout from the hangar as he pulled into the service yard. The old half-ton shot out of the hangar. Harold was driving and Angus slumped in the passenger seat. Harold spotted Jack and stopped.

"Come here, Jackie."

Jack jumped up on the running board of the truck.

"Get in beside him and press this against his side where he's bleeding." Harold handed Jack a large gauze compress from the first-aid kit.

Jack opened the door and squeezed in beside Angus, whose face was white as flour. Blood oozed from his left side through the shredded fabric of his coveralls. Jack placed the compress against the spot with his left hand and managed to close the door with his right.

"Just keep it pressed down," Harold said as he took off for the infirmary. "Might slow the bleeding."

"What happened?" Jack switched to holding the compress with his right hand stretched across Angus's body, trying not to touch his stomach and make things worse.

"Propeller," Harold said. "He was supposed to have all the switches off, and –"

"They were off," Angus said, his head still bent. "I'm sure they were."

"I came along in time to see him give the prop a good swing and all of a sudden the engine bursts into life and the prop rips through his coveralls."

Angus moaned.

"Hang on, man, we're there." Harold stopped the half-ton right in front of the doors and leaned on the horn. A startled orderly grabbed a stretcher and yelled for help. In a moment two guys sprinted to the truck as Jack and Harold helped Angus out of the cab. In another moment they had him settled on the stretcher and whisked him inside. Harold followed to explain what happened.

Jack shuddered. His hand was covered in blood and he tried to clean it off on the corner of the compress, which had fallen to the ground. He hoped Angus wasn't cut up too badly, hoped he'd soon be out of pain. He could easily have been sliced to pieces by the propeller, but Jack didn't think it would be that bad. Angus had still been conscious.

There had to be a better way of designing a plane. A guy shouldn't have to spin the propeller to get it going. He thought about the diagrams of the engine and propeller he'd studied in books and tried to see them in his mind. His fingers itched to hold a pencil and paper. He was sure he could think of something. Jack needed to learn a lot more, he knew that. Maybe he could work on that at university. Maybe he could come up with a new design and no one would ever have an accident like this one again.

Finally Harold came out the front door. "He's all right. Got some deep gashes that will need stitches and he'll have spectacular bruises, but they don't think there are any internal injuries. They're going to keep him in a couple of days till he starts to mend. Then he'll have to take it easy at home for a week or so."

Jack heaved a sigh of relief. Angus would be okay. There wouldn't be a new grave in the Cairn cemetery.

CHAPTER 15

The next Tuesday Wes and Jack tossed a baseball back and forth in front of the manse and the tidy white church. Jack told Wes what he had missed being away. He described Angus's accident.

"Could have been you, Jack."

"I know." Jack caught a fastball. "I'm not going to tell Mom."

"Meanwhile I just had to deal with homesick campers, skunks under the cabin and telling kids about God all week. That was a challenge."

"You wouldn't catch me doing that," laughed Jack. "That's your cup of tea, not mine, Reverend McLeod."

"Hey, knock it off, you…you science freak."

Cathy was swinging on the creaky wooden platform swing, watching for the old jalopy Trevor and Basil drove.

The three teens were waiting for Ivy to open the church door. She was inside, practicing her organ pieces for the church service. Ever since Basil and Trevor had shown up, Jack's mother had started playing more difficult music, like Bach.

Maybe she thought that if she could just get the music right, everything else would work out.

Jack shook his head, thinking of how hard it was to follow all Mom's rules and regulations for safety and security. His dad seemed to let her orders roll over him like a rain shower. But Jack couldn't. How was a guy supposed to grow up and spread his wings?

With a rattle and a roar, a car turned from the main street and headed up the hill. Trevor, Basil, and Buddy in the jalopy. Buddy, his head out the passenger side, started barking as the car stopped in front of the church. He leapt out and dashed up the lawn, throwing himself at Jack's knees, panting with excitement.

"Hi, old Buddy," Jack laughed. "Have you missed me?"

Jack visited Buddy most days during his lunch break, taking the dog a bit of meat and a slice of bread and butter and training him. Buddy knew how to sit, lie down, roll over, and shake a paw. He'd been growing like a bad weed, tripling in size in the last few weeks.

"Let's go, folks," Jack's mother called from the church porch, holding the door ajar. She saw Jack with the dog and shook her head in a gesture of disbelief, as if to say what a stubborn boy she had raised, but she didn't seem too upset, thank goodness.

Jack aimed a small grin in her direction, grabbed a rope from the back seat of the old car and tied Buddy to the fence.

The choir limbered up with scales, runs, oohs, aahs, stretches and arm waggles.

"Sit down everyone," Ivy said. Basil and Trevor had been singing with the choir for several weeks and now everyone knew each other well.

Jack tried not to look at Cathy too often.

"I don't blame you for admiring the scenery, Jack," Arnie whispered. "She's a fine looking girl."

Jack blushed beet red. He opened his music folder and tried to concentrate. Arnie, on one side of him, smelling of aftershave, hay and old clothes, sang a pure, sweet tenor and kept up a running commentary between verses. Trevor was on his other side, and Jack could see that he had something to tell him.

He got his chance as Ivy had the sopranos going over their part, with Cathy, who could sing any part, helping them.

"I went up today." Trevor whispered. "At first I was so scared of my instructor, I could hardly think about flying. He's a real stickler for procedure."

Jack was surprised. Trevor looked fearless. "The Tiger Moth's a pretty good crate," he said. And before he could think it through, he spoke. "I went up three months ago," he whispered.

Trevor looked impressed and Jack realized he couldn't stop now. "My sister's fiancé Sandy was a flying instructor."

"The one that's missing? The one your mother refers to all the time?"

Jack nodded.

"Did you like it?"

"It was swell. Sandy and I were up there most of the day."

"Tenors, could we have a little less chatter and a little more attention to the music," Ivy said. "From the beginning, please. Everyone."

Trevor was staring at Jack, really curious. Jack put his finger to his lips. He opened the music again and brought his eyes up to watch his mother as she played the accompaniment.

At tea break halfway through practice, Basil, Trevor, Cathy, Wes and Jack went out to the porch to get some fresh air. Cathy and Basil were talking heatedly about the music

MARY WOODBURY

for the fête. They wanted it to be different from the usual Sunday evening entertainments at the air base.

Basil and Cathy had far too much to say to each other, Jack thought, and he didn't like how close to each other they were standing.

"Aren't you worried about your sister?" he asked Wes, motioning at the two standing as close together as two pickets on the white fence around the manse.

"Basil's okay."

"Cathy might get her feelings hurt," said Jack. "He'll be gone in a couple of months."

"You're jealous, you idiot. Don't worry about Cathy, she can take care of herself."

Cathy and Basil joined them. "Let's drive over to Mortlach after," Cathy suggested.

"What for?" asked Wes. "There's nothing in Mortlach."

"Oh brother," laughed Jack. "How little you know." Then he whispered. "They just want to be together."

"Sounds like a great idea," said Basil. "I haven't been to Mortlach."

"We might need more gas," said Trevor. Gas rationing made everyone think twice about car travel. "The blokes who borrowed the jalopy last week only put a dollar's worth in."

"Will we all fit in the car?" asked Jack.

"Being crowded is half the fun," said Basil. "It's not a party without a proper gang."

"Seeing as I've been away, I've got a deadline for the base newsletter," said Wes. "I'm going to hit the typewriter."

Cathy studied her brother's face. "Are you sure?"

"I'll come the next time. I'm not that keen on ice cream anyway."

"Buddy loves ice cream," said Trevor. "Is there ice cream in Mortlach?"

Ivy struck three loud chords on the organ, and everyone hurried back to their spots.

"I don't think my mom will let me go," Jack whispered to Trevor. "She's suspicious of all moving vehicles."

"You've got to come," said Trevor. "To keep Buddy and I company. Basil and Cathy are becoming an item, if you hadn't noticed. He's been dropping into the administration office on the base ever since she started as a volunteer secretary."

"I can't stay out long." Jack had a hard enough time being in the same room as Cathy McLeod, let alone the same car. He was so jealous of Basil Skelton it wasn't funny. And he knew he didn't have a hope. Cathy was almost three years older than he was. But he couldn't help the way he felt.

His mother stared at him as he walked down the aisle to his seat. "We've still got work to do." Jack felt his stomach tighten.

"Turn to the new songbook and let's try 'Shine On Harvest Moon.' Tenors, you have a particularly interesting part." She peered over her glasses at Jack. "If you can pay attention, that is." Sometimes being the choir leader's son was as bad as being a PK. And now Arnie was whispering in his ear.

"My nieces say the old swimming hole is great these days. Maybe you should take those English boys out there for a good old Saskatchewan skinny dip. Just check that the girls aren't there before you chuck off your duds." He chuckled.

Jack whispered. "I'll warn them about the poison ivy close to the caragana, too." Jack had bad memories of itching and burning blotches of reddened skin when he was a kid. Flo had dosed him in calamine lotion and his mother had put Epsom salts in his bath.

After practice the four young people piled in the jalopy to head down the road to Mortlach. Ivy had repeated her "be careful" rant. "Don't drive fast. Get home by ten o'clock. Don't forget it's a workday tomorrow. Stop at the corners. Go slow past Hobbs' farm – their cat wanders at night and their old German shepherd sleeps on the road." Jack nodded in agreement. She had let him go, that was the main thing.

Trevor drove. Jack sat beside him. They stopped at the one-pump gas station for a dollar's worth of gas. Basil unscrewed the silver-coloured gas tank top while Trevor checked the oil. The jalopy needed a quart of oil every time it was filled with gas.

Frank, the older Boyle boy, worked the handle that pumped gasoline into the glass cylinder at the top. "That's about five gallons." Then he put the hose into the opening on the gas tank. Gravity fed the gas from the glass cylinder into the hose and then into the gas tank. Basil recapped the tank and Trevor banged the hood closed.

Trevor handed Frank a crisp dollar bill and gas ration coupons.

"How's the family doing?" Cathy leaned out to ask.

"Did you hear Jimmy tried to get into the army?" Frank asked. "They figured out he was too young right away. So he's back driving truck for Dad. Making deliveries to the Moose Jaw and Cairn airfields." He tucked the money in his pocket. "I'd join up myself but someone's got to keep an eye on the old man."

Cathy nodded. It wasn't often one of the Boyles talked this much.

"Where'd you get the dog?" Frank went on. "Looks like one of ours."

Basil and Trevor shrugged. Cathy and Jack said nothing.

"Jimmy's not too impressed with you, Jackie," Frank said. "I'd watch out for him. He's got a temper like Dad's."

"I know."

A few minutes later they were headed down the gravel road, dust clouds drifting behind them, the moon rising in the darkening sky. The last pencil-thin line of pinkish light faded on the western horizon. Soon the stars would be out. Crickets sang. Specks of light moved across the sky. Some of the RAF boys were doing night-flying exercises.

Basil and Cathy were singing "Coming In on a Wing and a Prayer" and laughing. Trevor was concentrating on driving. The brakes on the old Chevy weren't the best and the steering was loose as a hay wagon.

"The Moth's easier to steer than this bucket of bolts," Trevor said.

"I know," said Jack. "I mean, Sandy told me."

"Right, Jack," laughed Trevor. "You're a sly one."

"Don't know what you mean."

"Maybe one of these days I could take you up. Once I'm allowed to go solo, that is." Trevor dodged Hobbses' dozing German shepherd. "I guess your mom wouldn't approve of having a flyer for a son."

"She hates planes."

"My mom's a real softie," sighed Trevor. "It's Dad we have to worry about. He hit the roof when he found out I'd signed up. Threatened to throw me out of the house."

"What do you miss the most?"

"My two brothers – Terry, who's your age, and Tom, who's older."

"I only have a sister. But Wes is like a brother."

"I just hope Terry can stay out of Dad's way."

"My dad's a pussycat," laughed Jack. "Everyone likes him. He's not a very good businessman, though. If it weren't for the RAF coming in, we'd probably be out of business."

"Are you going to take over the store?"

"Me? Never."

"None of us wanted to work on the London docks like Dad. Tom can't, of course."

"Why can't he?"

"Run over by a horse and cart when he was nine."

"Oh."

"He takes care of the newsagent's shop on the corner. Terry delivers papers for him. Keeps it all in the family, you see. But Dad treats Tom like it was his brain that was injured, not his legs. I should be there to help but I ran off after the Blitz. After the bomb hit the house."

"Maybe Tom could find a place on his own."

"He needs help to do things."

The crew in the back seat was singing one song after another: "Waltzing Matilda," "There'll always be an England" and "The White Cliffs of Dover." The lights of Mortlach shone ahead.

"Maybe Tom will find a girl and get married."

"Mom would have a fit if he married at eighteen. She told us all to wait until we're twenty at least."

Jack was puzzled. Were Trevor and Tom twins? Could they be brothers and both eighteen? How long did it take to have a baby? "I thought you said Tom was older than you?"

"I mean nineteen. Tom's nineteen."

Trevor slowed down as they reached the outskirts of Mortlach. The whole town seemed to be sleeping. "That's what I meant to say. Tom's nineteen." And then he turned around. "Where to?"

"The café across from the grain elevator," said Cathy. "They make really good ice cream."

"Trevor?" Jack persisted. "How old are you?"

"Eighteen, of course. Chap has to be eighteen to be in the RAF." He pulled around the corner and stopped in front of the café.

"I think you skipped a year or two while you were growing up," said Jack with a grin on his face. "How'd you do it? Use Tom's birth certificate?"

Trevor grinned. "I wouldn't talk, Jackie boy. Just what did you do all those hours up in a Tiger Moth? Your mother would be pretty nervous if she knew."

"Okay, okay!"

Trevor put his index finger to his lips and led the group into the café. A few flyers sat with some Mortlach girls, otherwise the place was empty. The jukebox played Glenn Miller's "The Nearness of You." The group slid into a booth and ordered bowls of ice cream and cherry sodas.

Jack listened as they discussed going into Moose Jaw for an evening of dancing. As he watched, Cathy gave Basil a taste of her ice cream and Jack almost felt the cold silky cream run down his own throat. Maybe after Basil graduated and went back to England…

What a dreamer he was.

As they left the café, Trevor whispered, "Promise not to tell – about the age thing. I could get sent home."

"I'm good at keeping secrets." The two young men shook hands on it.

The drive home was much quieter. Jack pretended to fall asleep. He wouldn't even let himself think about Cathy and Basil.

No one sang any songs.

CHAPTER 16

One morning over a week later, Jack and Wes rode their bikes to the air base. Wes was working on the *Moth Monthly*, the base newsletter. He pointed to the sky.

"Looks like some of the guys are doing manoeuvres. You'd really like to be up there, wouldn't you?"

"I'd love to fly, you know that." Jack pointed at his big glasses and shook his head.

"Why do you need super eyesight to fly? There's nothing to bump into up there."

"There is over France and Germany. There's ack-ack around you and flak coming from the ground guns." Jack dodged a dead gopher.

"You'd fit right in, though. Me, I'm more like Cathy. I just want countries to figure out how to live together. I want to write for a newspaper, and not be a war correspondent."

"Wes, someone's got to put Hitler and Mussolini out of business."

"I know. Dragons have to be slain, but I don't want to do it," said Wes.

"If I was old enough, I'd go."

"I know."

Above their heads small planes banked, rolled and dived. Wes changed the subject. "Dexter and Cheese are afraid they might wash out. Cheese gets nosebleeds and makes mistakes. Dexter keeps gaining weight."

"Trevor loves it," Jack said. "And Basil feels right at home in the sky."

"Cathy's afraid for him," Wes said. "Basil takes chances. Pushes the limits. That's why she's so gaga about him."

"We should take Trevor and Basil out to the swimming hole at the farm, Dexter and Cheese too," Jack suggested as they pedalled onto the base.

"Maybe after work if they're free." Wes parked in front of the administration office. Jack headed across the pavement to the hangar and stuck his bike in the rack before heading to work. Harold and some of the younger mechanics were already there.

"About time you got here. Your dog's already curled up on his blanket waiting for you. LAC Knight dropped him off on his way to his flying lesson. He's going solo for the third time."

For a second Jack envied Trevor like crazy. Then he let it go.

Jack tucked his lunch in his locker and tugged on his coveralls and work boots. Buddy leapt to his feet as Jack strolled toward his workspace. He knelt and played with Buddy, made him sit, shake hands and play dead. He filled Buddy's water bowl and tossed some dog food in his dish. "You may hang out with all sorts of guys, Buddy, but you're still my dog, and don't you forget it."

Buddy cocked his head and the way his jaw was set, anyone looking would have sworn the dog was smiling.

"Enough, Jackie." Harold wiped sweat from his broad forehead as he came over. "I want you to wash down those two Moths to the left of the runway. Check if their bodies need any repairs. And stay clear of traffic. The flyboys are up and down like yo-yos. The instructors are shell-shocked from so many close calls and rescue missions."

"How's Angus?" Jack asked.

"Says he's healing fast. I'll put him on light duty for a few weeks."

Just then Jimmy Boyle pulled up in his dad's second truck. "Where do you want these oil drums?" he asked Harold. Then he saw Jack and shook his fist at him.

"Jack, take the tractor and show the young man where to stow the drums," said Harold.

Jack climbed on the tractor. "Follow me." He steeled himself for a confrontation.

He headed around the hangar to the shed at the side where the oil drums were stored, his heart beating fast. Wes wasn't there to intimidate Jimmy with his size. Jack couldn't run away or dodge him. He'd have to face him.

"So, Jackie boy?" Jimmy climbed down from the truck cab. "You've given those snooty British flyers a dog of mine. You've got the job I wanted – just because your dad owns a store, and now you're going to stand there and tell me where to stow this stuff." He unloaded an oil drum.

"I'll help unload." Jack strode to the back of the truck and started unloading drums and rolling them into the shed. His hands shook.

"Thanks for nothing, Foureyes!" Jimmy shouted Jack's old nickname from elementary school. "I'll deal with you in a minute."

"Look, Jimmy," Jack tried to sound calm, "I found that pup out on the roadside beside his dead mother. I got the job because Harold hired me. He doesn't even know my dad."

Jimmy raised his muscled arms and shoved Jack against the wall of the shed. The wood rattled and creaked. Jack lifted his arms to block the punch, but Jimmy pulled one of Jack's arms down and landed a right jab on his jaw. Jack twisted away and tripped Jimmy in the process. Dust rose. A crow squawked.

Jimmy jumped up quickly. "That was for getting me into trouble with my dad over the dogs. This one's for getting the job I wanted." He punched Jack again, this time on the nose. Jack felt blood spurt and saw a fountain of red stars.

He wrestled Jimmy to the ground. The two boys rolled and heaved on the gravel. Jack figured he was at least keeping Jimmy from getting in another punch.

"You're a stuck-up son-of-a-gun," Jimmy hollered. "Your brains can't help you now."

"You're a bully!" yelled Jack.

"Jackass!"

"Idiot!"

Jimmy got an arm free and Jack knew Jimmy was going to hit him again if he didn't get a punch in first. With the strength of desperation he sent a quick jab into Jimmy's face. With any luck, Jimmy was going to have a black eye.

"What's going on here?" Harold pulled up in the forklift.

Jack and Jimmy got to their feet. Jack brushed his coveralls and swabbed his bleeding nose with his hankie. He glanced sideways at Jimmy, who was rubbing his face. "It was nothing."

"Looked like a fight to me," said Harold.

Jimmy clambered into the truck cab in no time. He gunned the motor and pulled away.

"What was that all about?"

"Jimmy Boyle and I go back a long way." Jack sighed. "Buddy came from their bitch. Jimmy left him by the road to die." His whole head hurt. "I don't understand the way his mind works. Someone else is always to blame for everything."

"Doesn't want to take responsibility," Harold commented.

"I'm the opposite. I always figure, anything goes wrong, must be my fault." Jack rolled the last of the drums into the shed. "Thanks for coming along when you did."

"You were holding your own, Jackie Waters."

Jack couldn't help himself. He grinned sheepishly, closed the shed door and climbed back on the tractor.

Harold called after him, "You better go clean yourself up. Your face is a mess."

CHAPTER 17

Jack drove back to the front of the maintenance shop. He cleaned up as best he could in the dinky washroom, then picked up his cleaning supplies and walked out to the planes. Buddy trotted along with him and headed over to his favourite place by the fence to keep an eye on things.

Jack set to work. He knew Tiger Moths inside and out by now. He remembered the thrill of flying with Sandy and he remembered the tight fit of the cockpit. These days, he was scribbling in a notebook whenever he had a moment, trying to work out his ideas for improving the handling of controls in small planes, and maybe enlarging the cockpit as well. It would also be good if they could figure out a way to put a decent heater inside a small plane. A pilot nearly froze in wintertime. Next time he was in Moose Jaw, he'd see if the public library had books on aeronautics that he hadn't already seen at the base library.

If he couldn't be a pilot like Sandy, maybe he could be an aeronautical engineer and design better planes, safer planes. It was a land job. His mom would like that.

He washed down the cockpit of 5808 first, cleaned the dead bugs off the canopy and moved to work on the wings, watching for any rips in the fabric or bent bits that needed straightening.

Jack ran his hand over the smooth surface of the wing tip, caressing it as if it were alive. He loved these little yellow planes. He resonated with the way they worked, felt alive when he was around them. Imagine designing them, building them, testing them and then watching them fly – a man could really feel his life was worth something if he could do that. How big could you make them, how small, how safe and how easy to fly?

He lifted his hand off the smoothly stretched canvas wing and knew that, whatever he did with his life, it had to make him feel connected, focused like this.

He was nearly finished the first plane when he heard the horn sounding. He looked up in time to see two Ansons coming in for a landing at the same time, the top one coming in at a much steeper angle than the other. A jeep roared onto the runway, the ambulance revved its motor. Staff and maintenance personnel waved flags and shouted.

The top plane attempted to abort the approach and head up for a second pass but it didn't have the airspeed to climb out. The lower plane wavered like a butterfly with floppy wings just beneath it. Jack couldn't take his eyes off the scene.

The upper plane couldn't climb. The lower one probably didn't even know there was anything the matter. After all, the flyer below couldn't see the plane above him. But he must have just felt something land on him. The top plane had somehow managed to snag the top of the wings of the lower plane. They weaved back and forth, heading straight toward the hangar. Both of them must have been braking as best they could, but the top one had no control over anything. If it weren't so serious it would have been funny, thought Jack. It was one for the books.

Sirens wailed, horns blared, Buddy barked and a crowd gathered at the fence away from the open doors of the hangar.

Jack scrambled off the Moth he was working on and ran out to join the spectators. Ten feet from the hangar door, the planes came to a skidding stop. The smells of rubber and gas floated on the dust in Jack's direction.

The two pilots were hauled from the planes and marched away toward the administration office. Harold and the other mechanics raced to separate the two planes and check that there was no danger of fire.

Harold beckoned Jack over. "We need coffee, Jackie boy. Gotta figure out how to get these two lame birds apart. It's a good question whether these planes will ever fly again or if we have to write them off. It's going to be a heck of a job. I never cared for Ansons anyway."

"I've never seen anything like that in my whole life," said George, an older mechanic from the night shift who was filling in for Angus. "And I worked at Blatchford Field in Edmonton for years."

"I wish Angus was here. This is going to take a lot of work." Harold strode up and down, growling about the whole dilemma. "We aren't miracle workers."

"Those two students are lucky to be alive. Especially the one on the top," said another mechanic, sitting on the floor with motor parts surrounding him. "He came in too steeply. The other bloke never knew what hit him."

"That top flyer will wash out for sure. He'll be off to Observer School, I bet," Harold said.

"Who were they?" Jack asked.

"Dexter and Cheese." Harold glanced at the list of pilots. "Who else?"

Jack took the thermos and headed to the canteen. He passed Basil and Cathy walking on the path between the small airport store and the admin office, sharing a bottle of soda.

"What happened to your face, Jack?" asked Cathy.

Jack shrugged. He'd forgotten all about his scrap with Jimmy Boyle in all the excitement. He'd cleaned away the blood, although his jaw still ached and his nose throbbed. But he'd held his own.

Basil and Cathy had seen the two planes come down. "Who was it?" she asked.

"Cheese and Dexter," Jack said. "They're okay, and we'll know about the planes in a bit."

"They're lucky they walked away," laughed Basil. "That was some fancy manoeuvring."

As he headed into the mess, Jack heard Cathy speaking firmly to Basil. "I don't want you trying any stunts like that."

"Don't worry, darling girl. With the future we've got planned, I won't risk anything I don't have to." He bent and kissed her lightly on the cheek.

Watching the two lovebirds, Jack's mood dipped below zero. So much for first love, Foureyes. He got the coffee and went back to his planes. Buddy chewed on a bone the cook had sent him and watched as the repair crews worked at prying the two Ansons apart. It was going to take a long time to repair those trainers, that was for sure.

At lunch Wes showed Jack the cartoon he'd drawn of two planes on top of each other – "Coming in on a wing and a flyer," he'd written under the line drawing. His artwork wasn't much but his ideas were great.

"Do you think the newsletter committee will let you print it?"

Wes shrugged. "Probably not."

Cathy and Basil, with Trevor trailing behind them, came over to where the two boys were sitting on the grass in front of the mess. "I say, how about we all skedaddle into Moose Jaw tonight to celebrate Dexter and Cheese's miraculous escape," Basil said.

"We were thinking of going swimming at the Hobbs farm," said Wes.

Trevor glanced at Basil. "We'd thought about going to Moose Jaw earlier. The thing with Dexter and Cheese just made up our minds."

"I've got a little business to attend to in the city." Basil grinned.

"And Jack can fill us in on his bruises," said Trevor.

"How will we get there?" Jack asked. "We can't all fit in the jalopy."

"Maybe you could borrow your dad's truck," said Cathy. "I've seen you drive. A carton of fresh eggs would be safe with you."

Jack smiled. So Cathy thought he was a good driver. But then why did she fall for Basil, the guy who took risks?

"What about gas?" Wes asked.

"No problem." Basil patted his wallet. "I've got it covered."

"I have to be back by ten o'clock."

"Jackie, leave it to us." Trevor said. "We're not raw recruits – we've dealt with sergeants and curfews before."

"My mother's tougher than any sergeant," laughed Jack.

At five to one everyone headed back to work. Basil and Trevor had an exam on airmanship. "Okay, Jackie, tell me about the centre of gravity," teased Trevor as they walked back toward the hangar and the school.

"The centre of gravity is the point in a body through which the resultant of the weight of its parts passes, in every position that it can assume."

"Have you memorized the textbooks?" asked Basil.

"Nearly."

Trevor chuckled. "Do you understand what it means?"

"I think so. When a plane turns, it rotates around its centre of gravity. That's why it's important for a pilot to know where the centre of gravity of his plane is." Jack pointed to Harold's quarter-ton truck. "On the ground, a truck has more weight higher up than a jalopy, so its centre of gravity is higher."

"Bravo!" Trevor said. "I still don't get it, but I will before the exam."

"Too bad you're not eighteen, Jack," said Basil. "I'd take you up with me anytime. You'd probably be a great navigator."

"Thanks. I'd go in a minute."

The two young pilots sauntered away, leaving Jack to go back to work.

Jack was struck by an odd thought. The centre of gravity of his world had shifted – from Cairn village and the church, store and home, to the flying school and beyond. No wonder he felt pulled.

He was afraid for Sandy and Flo and the threat to the world he knew. Then again, Dr. McLeod had said that fear was the beginning of wisdom.

Jack had seen a small corner of that fear this very morning, facing Jimmy Boyle. He'd stood up for himself. But he didn't feel particularly wise yet.

CHAPTER 18

Later that afternoon, as Jack was cleaning up, Trevor came into the shop.

"Looks like Cheese is washing out. He got called on the carpet this afternoon. It was his second problem flight. He'd been warned before but never told us. He'll be shipped out to a school for navigators."

"How's he doing?"

"Pretty broken up. We've been together since basic training, the four of us."

"Anything I can do?" asked Jack. He couldn't begin to imagine how devastated Cheese would be.

"Well, we better have a really good party tonight in Moose Jaw."

"We'll hit all the hot spots." Jack laughed. Not that he'd be able to go into beer parlours or the like. He'd leave that to the older guys.

"I've been thinking. I should be able to take you up in the next week or so, if you're game."

"What if we get caught? Wouldn't you get washed out too?"

"Well, we just can't get caught." Trevor headed for the door.

Jack, Wes and Cathy and the four airmen piled into the jalopy and headed into Cairn after work, with Cathy on Basil's lap and Dexter and Cheese perched on top of Wes, who complained about his legs going to sleep under the weight.

Jack went into the store and asked his parents for the loan of the truck. "I could pick up supplies at the wholesaler at the same time," he suggested.

Ivy said no. Bill said yes.

"What happened to your face?" his mother asked as she walked toward the storeroom at the back of the store.

"I fell getting off the tractor." Sort of true, he thought, except he'd had help falling. Mom pursed her lips but didn't comment.

"That's quite a bruise," his dad reflected as Ivy moved out of earshot. "Looks more like a punch to the nose." He sat on the captain's chair with his feet up on a milk crate. "Who did it?"

Jack mouthed, "Jimmy Boyle," and his dad nodded.

Bill Waters got up slowly and headed toward the back of the store. "I'll talk to your mother, Jack. We do need supplies. Give me a couple of minutes."

Jack went out to the porch where the other young people stood talking to Arnie and Mel Hobbs about the trip to town.

"I hear the townies and the air force have been mixing it up," Arnie said.

"Yeah," Mel said, "seems the town fellas think the airmen have taken all the beautiful girls."

Jack thought of Basil and Cathy. He knew one flyer who had the best girl in his village.

"You watch out while you're in town. I mean it," Mel went on.

"And remember, Jackie boy," said Arnie, serious for a change, "courage is not a gift: courage is a decision."

Jack nodded. "I'll try to remember that."

"Looks like Jackie's been in a bit of a brawl himself," laughed Mel.

Jackie warned the twins not to say anything and told his story about his confrontation with Jimmy Boyle.

Finally Jack's parents came out to give their permission plus an extension of his curfew to eleven p.m., seeing as he was going to get supplies for the store. Mom started her safety lecture and Bill handed out liquorice twists. Dexter and Cheese strolled back from the pharmacy. Cheese looked really glum. He and Dexter climbed into the back seat of the jalopy with Wes, behind Basil and Cathy. They left first. It seemed that Basil was in a hurry, as usual. Jack climbed into the truck's narrow seat and Trevor sat on the passenger side, having moved the pile of candy wrappers, mail and bills from the seat. The truck was Jack's dad's responsibility, so it was not the tidiest.

Jack headed east down Railway Avenue toward Moose Jaw.

"I was thinking about home," Trevor said. "London is a great city, full of bustle and business, but there's something special about a small place like this." He took out his meteorology notes to study for a test the next day. "I'm going to miss Cairn – your mother's cooking, you and Wes."

For some reason Jack felt a lump in his throat. He put his foot on the gas to pass a hay wagon. He needed to get a move on – Basil had driven off and disappeared down the highway before Bill had finished giving Jack directions and a cheque for the wholesaler. The two carloads were meeting at the Ambassador Café for supper at 6:30 p.m.

Trevor put away his notes. "Why don't we plan our trip? I can land at the emergency field at Bushell Park. You can drive Sandy's car and meet me there. We'll go for a spin in a Moth. It'll be a lark."

Jack hesitated. His mother would have a fit if she ever found out.

"You want to go up again, don't you?"

"What do you think?"

"It's a deal, then." Trevor caught a fly on the wing and tossed it out the window.

Jack drove to the wholesaler's first. Trevor helped Jack load the cartons of tinned foods and cereals, along with wooden crates of soda and packets of candy. They threw a canvas tarp over the boxes and tied it down.

"Haven't seen your dad for a while," said the owner as Jack paid the invoice.

"His back's acting up. Mom's running things for now."

"I don't think your dad really likes retail. Wasn't he a travelling salesman first?"

"I don't know. I was only five when Grandpa died and Dad took over the store."

"Old Waters was a fine fellow. He sure was broken up when his oldest son came home from the war the way he did. Don't think he ever got over it."

"You mean Uncle Jack or Grandpa?"

"Both of them. That young man had seen too much. Must have been hard on Ivy. Such a lively girl. Talented too, and pretty as a picture. A Chautauqua girl. I heard her sing, did she tell you?"

His mother, a lively girl, a real beauty? Jack couldn't believe his ears. This big, bald man with thick arms, sporting a tattoo on his right bicep, knew more about his family than he did.

"She plays the organ and leads the choir at the United Church."

"Jack played the piano and saxophone, did you know that? They played duets until he went to war."

Trevor honked the horn of the old truck. Jack hesitated, took the receipt from the guy and turned to go. He had a mass of questions skittering around his brain like a bucket of baseballs dumped on the diamond during practice.

"It was a shame what happened."

"Yeah, it was." He didn't have the nerve to tell the guy he didn't know what had happened and he was afraid to ask. What you don't know can't hurt you. That's what his dad would say.

"What took you so long?" Trevor asked. "Was that fellow telling you his life story or something?"

Jack didn't answer.

CHAPTER 19

As they drove to the Ambassador, Trevor pointed out Basil and Cathy coming out of Plaxton's Jewellers. "I bet he's popped the question," Trevor said.

"What?"

"Basil said he was going to ask Cathy to marry him after the war." Trevor hooted. "This calls for a real celebration."

Well, that's the end. Your first romance, Jackie boy, and the girl doesn't even know you're alive. Then she goes and falls for the first handsome flyer she meets. He chewed his lips and kept his eyes on the road.

"I think all of us fell for Cathy. Basil's a lucky bloke." Trevor glanced at Jack's brooding focus on the road. "Where's this restaurant?"

When they pulled up in front of the Ambassador, Cheese and Dexter were standing on the sidewalk smoking cigarettes. "About time you guys got here," Dexter said. "Wes headed to the newsstand. We've lost track of the other two. We've been to Eaton's and the Army & Navy. I bought a white silk scarf for graduation."

Cheese ground his cigarette out with a vengeance. "I won't be needing one."

Just then Basil and Cathy came around the corner holding hands and grinning like Cheshire cats. "Sorry!" said Basil. "We got busy."

Cathy showed everyone her diamond ring. It must have cost a bundle. It was big and shiny. Jack pretended a lack of interest. He sure didn't see himself giving a girl a ring, not for a long time.

Basil pulled out an Eaton's box and opened it with a great flourish. "I may not get a ring but I get a real flyer's scarf." He wrapped it around his neck and twirled Cathy in his arms. "This is the happiest day of my life so far," he laughed. "Getting my wings will pale beside marrying this fabulous woman."

After much backslapping and hugging, they went into the restaurant. Wes came in a few minutes later and joined them in a booth. He waved a pile of comic books and magazines at Jack.

"I'll let you borrow these when I'm done."

"Look what your big sister got." Cathy leaned across and waved her ring under her little brother's face. "What do you think?"

"Great! Congratulations!"

There was a sudden burst of chatter and laughter from the rest of the crowd around the table.

Jack didn't say anything. No one seemed to notice.

Jack and Wes had hot beef sandwiches awash in gravy, French fries, and mushy green peas. Dexter tried the liver and onions, but it was tough. Everyone else had the Chinese dinner special. They didn't have dessert because they were going down the street to Johnstone Dairies for ice cream.

A half an hour later the whole gang sauntered down the street licking ice cream cones. Cathy, Basil, Dexter and Cheese went off to a dance at Temple Gardens.

Trevor, Jack and Wes were going to the Capitol theatre to see a Western. The group would reconvene outside the CPR station at 10 p.m. and make their way home in tandem in case either car had trouble.

The movie let out about nine-thirty.

"Let's shoot billiards," suggested Trevor.

"I don't know how," said Jack. He sounded cranky. The movie hadn't made him feel any better. There'd been too much kissing for his liking. He had wanted cowboy action.

Wes said. "You can teach us, Trevor. It might cheer up our disappointed lover boy."

Jack punched Wes's arm. "I'm no lover boy."

Trevor led the way to the Connaught Billiard Hall. "We had a couple of tables in the mess in basic training. I got pretty good."

The place was full of smoke, and strong lights hung over the four green tables. Several workmen stood clutching pool cues. A couple of young guys were matched at the nearest table.

"I didn't know we let in the RAF," said the one who was poised to take a shot. "Or should I call them riff-RAF?"

Jack picked his way through the gloom toward an empty table.

"Look at that, Repete. Look what the cat dragged in," shouted Jimmy Boyle, standing up in the shadows. "It's PK and Foureyes."

"Yah, look at what the cat dragged in."

"Looks like you ran into some trouble," hollered Jimmy.

"You ran into trouble, Jackie. Jimmy says you stole his dog."

"I didn't steal his dog," shouted Jack. "I saved the pup's life. Jimmy left him to die."

"Haven't you had enough yet?" Jimmy asked.

"Yeah, Jackie, haven't you had enough?" Repete stomped right up to Jack, close enough so that Jack could smell stale sweat and beer breath.

"Take it outside, boys. This is a respectable place." The owner opened the front door and ushered them all out. The younger players had joined Jimmy and Repete as they filed out.

"Fight! Fight!" one guy called.

Jack stood with clenched fists. "I don't want to fight any more, Jimmy. You didn't want the dog anyway. This is stupid."

"Did you call me stupid?"

"No, I didn't."

"Yes, you did," said Repete. "I heard you."

"Butt out of it, Repete," Jimmy said.

Meanwhile a scuffle had started between one of the labourers and an RAF flyer.

Just then the jalopy pulled up to the curb. "What's going on?" Basil jumped out. Dexter and Cheese followed. Cathy stepped carefully away from the car and the fracas.

"None of your business, Limey." Repete put both his fists up into a boxer's pose. "Back off, if you know what's good for you."

"What's all this then?" a group of RCAF men came strolling down the street from the closest hotel bar. "Someone picking on our friends?"

A couple of Repete and Jimmy's friends turned and shouted at the group of nattily dressed airmen. "You guys come in here thinking you're God's gift to the universe. This is our town. Why don't you go home?"

A sergeant with huge shoulders and a thick Yorkshire accent was holding Repete Nelson. "We'll have none of that, now." Repete was struggling to break free. The sergeant pulled him closer, one huge arm wrapped around the boy's upper chest and neck.

Repete opened his mouth but no sounds came out.

"Keep your trap shut, boyo."

"The Cairn babies have their pet flyers with them," hollered one of Jimmy's friends.

Trevor stepped into the fray. "You got something against flyers, kid?"

The town guy's fist connected with Trevor's jaw. Trevor grabbed him in his wiry arms and put his left leg out to trip the burly kid. The two fighters toppled over.

Before anyone could stop it, a regular wrestling match was underway as the townie and Trevor rolled on the cement sidewalk. The crowd split between townies and the military. Shouts filled the once-quiet night air.

A fat youth smashed a bottle and held it out menacingly. A scuffle broke out between two well-built LACs and a couple of construction workers. A crowd of supporters screamed and taunted from the sidelines. Traffic slowed on the street.

Two police cars slid to a stop across the street.

"Break it up!" someone yelled. "They'll haul us all to jail."

"Come on, Trevor," yelled Jack.

Jimmy Boyle strolled over. "So, Jackie boy, are we even?"

"For now, I'd say so," said Jack.

"Nothing like a good fight, Jack," Jimmy chuckled.

"Speak for yourself. I'm the one with bruises." But he thought he could see a shiner around Jimmy's left eye where he'd got in one good punch.

"See you around." Jimmy moved to the sidelines. "Take good care of my dog, you hear." He and Repete moved off.

The Cairn crew broke away and ran down the lane to the old truck parked near the CPR station and clambered in. Cathy, Basil and Trevor squeezed into the cab and the rest jumped in the back with the groceries. Jack hopped into the driver's seat and drove off.

"Did you see the size of the sergeant that held Repete?" asked Jack.

"What about those two goons that took on the RCAF boys?" asked Basil.

"They're both gonna have bruises tomorrow," commented Jack.

"No worse than yours," laughed Trevor. "Did Jimmy say anything to you before he and Repete ran off?"

"He says we're even now."

"Good," suggested Cathy. "It's over."

"We'll see," said Jack.

"What about the jalopy?" Basil asked. "We should go back for it."

"I wouldn't advise going back for anything," said Trevor. "There will be military police and town cops all over the place."

"Let's keep going," Jack said. "I've got to get this stuff home."

Cathy sat on Basil's lap by the passenger window. "Two guys smashed the front window of the jalopy while you were fighting. I was glad I'd gotten out."

Jack concentrated on driving through the quiet streets to the highway, his heart racing. He kept his eye on the rearview mirror to see if any police cars were following.

"Some Farewell-to-Cheese party, some engagement party," Cathy said. "Let's go home. I want to show Mom and Dad my ring." She waved her left hand in front of her.

Dexter knocked on the back window of the cab. He shouted, "Slow down, will you? This isn't the most comfortable place to sit." Wes, Dexter and Cheese were perched on cartons and crates from the wholesaler's in the back of the truck.

Jack took a deep breath and eased his foot onto the brake. No sense being stopped by the RCMP. He waved at Dexter through the dusty back window.

"Those townies have been spoiling for a fight ever since the first trainees arrived," said Trevor, sitting in the middle, trying not to get in Jack's way as he changed gears. "Doesn't scare me. I was raised on a street of brawlers."

I wasn't, thought Jack. I was raised in a house full of rules.

"Small wars, big wars, they're all the same," Trevor continued. "It's about power and control. Bullies and victims. We all have to decide where we stand. This afternoon Jack stood up for Buddy, tonight I stood up for the military." Jack focused his attention to the dark road, but Trevor's words pleased him.

Jack decided he'd drop the airmen off first, then Cathy and Wes, and then take the truck back to the store.

He had a few questions to ask his dad.

CHAPTER 20

I t was eleven o'clock but Jack's parents were sitting on the front porch of the store watching for him. Something about their silence cut off greeting and conversation. Wes and Cathy headed home without stopping to talk. Cathy wanted to show her parents the ring before anyone else in town saw it. But Jack told his folks.

His mother shook her head. His dad motioned for Jack to sit down on the step.

"I should put the stuff away."

"It can wait."

Jack wondered whether someone had reported to his folks about the fight in Moose Jaw. No one from Cairn could have seen them, could they? And why were they sitting here instead of at home?

"We received a telegram from Flo's supervisor." His

mother was talking so quietly that Jack had to strain to hear her words. "Flo's been wounded. She's in the hospital."

Jack felt as if a brick had hit him in the stomach. "Is she going to be all right?"

His dad took over. "They didn't say much. Just that her injuries are being treated and…she's in critical condition."

"What happened? Was the hospital hit?"

"We don't know," said his dad.

"I kept thinking of her last letter where she said she had enjoyed her leave by the sea. She was looking forward to going hiking with friends." His mother was gripping her lace hankie as if it was a life preserver.

"Yeah," said Jack. Maybe Flo had really been shipped out to a field hospital as he had suspected when he read that bit of news. Could you get wounded in a hospital in England? He tried to concentrate on the conversation.

"Remember, she said all sorts of military bands were on parade. And that she thought her dad would have liked it, seeing as he'd played the saxophone." Bill stretched his feet out in front and rubbed his hands along the sides of his trousers.

"She thanked me for the music lessons," Ivy said.

Did Flo think she wouldn't have another chance? Jack asked himself.

"Flo will be all right," said Jack. "She's made of tough stuff."

"Time will tell." Ivy sighed and rose as slowly as an old woman. "I'm going home."

"I'll help Jack unload."

"Don't throw your back out any worse than it is," Ivy said over her shoulder. "Jack, you lift the heavy stuff." Then she was gone.

Jack drove the truck behind the store and his dad opened the storeroom door. They unloaded quickly. Then his dad opened two root beers and they sat back down on the porch.

"How was your day, Jack?"

Jack told his father all the funny and not-so-funny things that had happened at the base and in Moose Jaw.

"Holy cow!"

Jack smiled briefly. "That ought to give you enough stories for a week, Dad. Except maybe you better not tell them."

"Probably not." Bill sighed and stretched his long legs in front of him again, stared at his shoes. "Do you think Flo was near the front lines?"

"I think that's what her letter was hinting."

"I'm glad your mother didn't make the connections."

"You and Flo and I were always the ones for puzzles."

"We will be again, Jack." Bill stood up. "Shall we go home?"

"I've got a couple of questions. But if it's not the right time…"

"I'm not going to sleep, anyway, so shoot."

Jack hesitated. He didn't want to upset his dad any more than he was, but his need to understand his family was stronger than his worry.

"How did Uncle Jack die? The guy at the wholesalers knew more about it than I did. I'm not a kid anymore."

"No, you're not, Jack." His dad sat down again. There was a longer silence than usual. Bill seemed to be gathering himself together to make a statement. "I've been trying to find the right words, the right time to tell you this story. It's not easy to talk about.

"Every family has a few things they don't talk about. Some tragedy or sadness, some unresolved problem they don't want seen. Families have a hard enough time dealing with living in a small town, being a member of a particular family, having one or another of their family members act other than 'normal.'"

Jack rubbed his sore jaw. He knew what it was like living in Cairn, being a Waters. He had a reminder of that. He drained his soda pop.

Jack's dad walked down the steps of the store and crossed Railway Avenue to the rail yard. "Your Uncle Jack, my big brother, came home from the Great War in one piece. He flew with Wop May, the famous Alberta bush pilot, you know." Jack put the two empty root beer bottles in the wooden crate by the door and caught up with his dad.

"His body was fine," Bill Waters continued. "But my brother was always a moody guy, even as a boy. He was energetic, musical, talented, not as outgoing as me. He was the family charmer. I was the joker. Our dad made a lot of him. He was so proud."

"Then he met Mom," Jack said.

"Jack and Ivy made a great couple. It was a love match from the first date."

"Where were you?"

"I got a job right after high school as a traveller. I had southern Alberta and Saskatchewan as my territory and I loved the open road – visiting schools, factories and businesses, selling cleaning products. I was West Chemicals' top salesman. I knew where all the best pickles, Ukrainian sausage and pyrogies were sold, where the best cheese was made. And I'd bring them home to my father and mother."

Bill wandered along beside the train tracks with Jack beside him until he came to the level crossing with its crisscrossed white warning signs.

"No one knows for sure whether it was an accident or suicide."

Jack stood with his hands in his pockets, listening to the sound of an approaching freight. He felt a slight hum from the track beneath his feet. He stepped back a few paces onto the gravel approach.

"Jack had never been a drinker before the war. When he came home he was. He'd never been a loudmouth. In 1919 he was. It was like he was ashamed of surviving. He'd lived and his best friends had died. But something inside him *had* died. The whole family went into shock. We tried to cover up for him, tried to protect Ivy. After all, he was a war hero, a pilot. He was my brother. And they were expecting a baby, for God's sake."

Bill took a deep breath. "One night Jack didn't come home from Moose Jaw. Dad went out looking for him. As he backed his truck onto the street he heard the midnight express from Regina to Calgary blow its warning whistle. There were screaming brakes, shouting trainmen and a loud bang."

Jack gulped a lungful of air. The night train pulled through town, wheels clicking against the track. Its dark form, like a ghost train, cut off the view of the other side of the road.

"He was killed instantly, Doc said. Jack's buried beside Grandma and Grandpa. Everyone in town has their own theory about what happened that night, but they've learned to keep it to themselves. We all have."

"I'm sorry."

"We should have told you sooner. But I was raised in a family that didn't talk about personal things. I don't know anything about the Waters family before my dad. Sometimes I think I tell stories to make up for the stories I never heard and the one story I can't talk about. Does that sound stupid?"

Jack touched his dad's arm. "No."

"Good. I'd hate to think you thought your old man was stupid. Can you believe it, my dad and the teacher wanted me to go to university? I went for one year just to please them and flunked out. I don't think it was lack of brains. I just couldn't imagine sitting still, reading books all day, writing papers, studying for exams for four years."

Jack chuckled. That was where he and his dad differed. He could hardly wait for the challenge. He'd design a safer plane – safer and faster – one with a self-starting propeller and no way for it to land on top of another kite.

"Ivy was alone with that wee baby. I came home and saw the lay of the land. It wasn't hard to fall in love with the most talented musician in the district. I was tired of sowing my wild oats anyway."

Jack discovered he had a lump in his throat the size of a golf ball. He didn't say anything.

"Losing a brother is really hard, Jack. I'm glad you'll never have to go through that."

"Sandy was like an older brother," whispered Jack. "But I didn't know him my whole life."

The man and boy walked down the dark street together. Bill locked up the store but left the truck parked as it was. Crickets sang. An owl hooted. A bunch of coyotes howled in the distance. The smell of dew, fresh cut grass and watered flowers drifted toward them. They let themselves in the house and went to bed.

In his room Jack found his latest model airplane smashed on the floor. He'd left the window open and there'd been a stiff breeze earlier. He picked it up and put it on his desk in the corner. He'd have to repair it tomorrow.

The good news was, it was easily fixed.

Jack lay for a long time going over the whole day, the whole of his family history. Trust Dad to give him the straight goods. For an older guy he was pretty sharp. Why did knowing the facts make Jack feel better? He said a little prayer under his breath for Flo and Sandy and his mother and went to sleep.

He dreamt of flying high in a brand-new single-wing airplane all the way to England to save his sister.

The next day at the flying school the usual gang said good-bye to Cheese. Cathy hugged him. Jack and Wes shook his hand. Dexter, Trevor and Basil were in class. Cheese tried his best to grin and be a good sport. "Thanks for everything," he said. "Tallyho and all that." But the poor guy's face crumpled worse than the wing of Jack's model after it had fallen. None of them knew how to help.

Cheese marched off toward the H-hut with his head held high and his shoulders square.

CHAPTER 21
AUGUST 1943

The first few weeks of August flew by. Farmers ran tractors, workhorses pulled carts of hay and teenagers loaded forage onto wagons. The RAF boys flew solo and took exams in meteorology, airframe – everything you ought to know about the body of each plane – and the theory of flight.

The Cairn Cosmopolitan Music Society auditioned and selected the programme of musical, dance, comedy and recitation acts for the upcoming fête. Rehearsals were in full swing. Trevor and Basil listened to all the performers, made suggestions and sang with Wes and Jack as the star quartet. Jack was really proud of their close harmonies on songs like "We'll Meet Again," which always made him think of Flo and Sandy.

The men's chorus, with Mel and Arnie Hobbs and Howie Wong as well as a bunch of staff from the flying school, worked with Basil as their director and Trevor as accompanist. The choir had rehearsed a medley of catchy tunes. Cathy and Wes were playing a real duet, not "Chopsticks".

An undercurrent of excitement flowed through the village and on the airfield like a sweet spring of clear water. The British flyers tried the swimming hole a couple of times but they weren't as good in the water as they were in the air or on the stage.

Basil was to be the master of ceremonies, assisted by Dr. McLeod when Basil was performing. Trevor and Ivy were splitting the job of accompanying singers. Cathy was singing a duet with Rose, the oldest of the Hobbs girls from the farm.

One of the Link training staff had memorized a couple of comic monologues by a British actor called Stanley Holloway. Dexter would perform magic tricks. Incredibly, even the Boyles were getting into the spirit. They'd amazed everyone at the audition with their lively step dancing, accompanied by a fiddler from Mortlach. Even Jimmy had come and he'd actually seemed to enjoy it.

Jack's dad was going to whistle a trio of songs from the Great War. He had a special double whistle – two notes at once – a family tradition that Jack hadn't mastered. Bill had also written and would perform a comic monologue, mostly jokes from the *Reader's Digest*.

He tried them out on Ivy and Jack one night while Trevor and Basil were rehearsing with some of the other performers. Buddy had been allowed in the Waters' backyard for a visit. The family was sitting outside in their beat-up deck chairs.

"Ivy and I had words but unfortunately I never got to use mine… My feet were so cold in January that I was walking by memory… Did you hear about the RAF pilot who got lost flying around Saskatchewan? When he ran out of fuel he landed at the next air base. 'Sorry,' he said. 'I kept looking for the town of Cairn, but I must have been going in circles. I just kept crossing the town of Ogilvie. It said so on the green grain elevators.' 'Oh, you silly blighter, Ogilvie is the name of the grain company.'"

"I wish I could put Buddy on stage," said Jack. "He's so good at tricks he could be in a circus." He pulled a couple of burrs out of the dog's tail. "He can do more tricks than Dexter."

"I don't think Buddy wants to leave home yet," his dad chuckled. "He's not ready to go on the road like Ivy did."

Mom blushed. "I can't believe I did all that." Then she sat back in her chair, sipped her second cup of tea and told

Jack stories about what it had been like to travel with Chautauqua.

"We used to come barrelling into town an hour before the evening show, setting up flats on stage, pressing costumes, putting on greasepaint. Going onstage not knowing what kind of audience you were going to get. Usually the piano was out of tune. That drove me mad. One time a fire and brimstone preacher called me a shameless hussy. The local crowd told him to sit down and be quiet or leave. It was a great way to spend the summer."

Jack couldn't believe such a thing as Chautauqua had ever existed in Saskatchewan or that his careful, controlled mother had been part of it.

What had gotten into his mother? Here they were in the middle of the war, her daughter and future son-in-law were in trouble, and Mom was telling stories.

"You should write that down, Ivy," said Jack's dad.

"It's better hearing it first-hand," said Jack. He wished Flo and Sandy could hear too.

"I'll go pick up our dinner," suggested Dad.

"I'll go." Jack took the money that was sitting on the outdoor table and sprinted down the street.

Jack ran into Jimmy and Repete at Wong's. They were all picking up takeout chow mein and chicken balls. Jack broke the silence.

"That was some fight in Moose Jaw, eh?"

"Yeah." Jimmy shuffled his feet. "Good thing we all took off."

"Did any of your friends get arrested?"

"Nope." Repete shook his head. "None of our friends."

"My brother Frank is leaving for Calgary tomorrow," said Jimmy.

"There's lots of work there," said Repete.

"Repete and I are going after the concert," said Jimmy. "I'm tired of driving my dad's truck. He's too bossy."

Grouchy and a mean drunk is more like it, thought Jack. He didn't blame Jimmy for wanting to get away.

"Yeah, we're waiting until after the concert," echoed Repete. "My grandma needs help with stuff. She's in charge of decorating the hall." Repete had his hands in his worn trouser pockets. His eyes were on Jimmy all the time, taking his cues from his best buddy.

"You like those stupid Brit flyers, Jackie?" Jimmy fumbled with the cigarette packet in his shirt pocket. "Seem pretty stuck-up to me."

"They're all right. So I see you're dancing at the hall."

"Yeah, our whole family. It's an Irish thing. We haven't done it together for years."

"Sounds good. Me, I've got two left feet."

"That so?" Jimmy grinned. "You're not Irish, I guess."

"No."

"I guess you can't help it if you're a brain and have no useful skills."

Jack had to bite his tongue to stop himself from pointing to his assistant mechanic job at the air base, let alone the fact that he could fly a plane. He could feel his face flush, his fists clench. But it wasn't worth the trouble. Jimmy was just testing him. He let it go.

"Guess not," he said.

"Your order is ready, Jackie," said Howie. He was humming a song that the men's chorus was practicing under his breath as he handed over the brown bag, took the money and gave Jack change.

"See you at practice, Jimmy. You too, Mr. Wong."

The restaurant owner smiled.

"Yeah, see you." Jimmy went through the door and headed left to Pasqua Street.

Jack walked down the street and up the hill to his house. He was glad the Boyle siege was over. Jimmy was still a jerk and Jack knew enough to keep a lid on his expectations of a prolonged truce. The Boyles were like weather, unpredictable.

Jack and his parents dug into the Chinese food and talked about the upcoming concert. Everyone in the village was humming tunes, dancing jigs or preparing monologues. Even

Buddy seemed to get into the swing of things. His tail was in permanent wag as he followed Trevor, Basil or Jack around.

The next Saturday, Jack dressed carefully. He had the day off, the sky was blue and he had a mission and a destination. He crossed his fingers as he came down the hall to the kitchen.

"I'm going to take Sandy's car for a little spin, Dad. Then I'll bring it back and give it a good wash and wax before I put it away again."

"Sure wish we'd hear some news from overseas." Dad sipped tea and nibbled on a homemade cinnamon bun with raspberry preserves. Jack grabbed a bun too and gulped down a glass of milk. His mom was in a baking frenzy these days. Maybe it helped keep the worries at bay.

"I'll be home for lunch," said Jack casually.

"That's some spin you're going on then." His dad peered over the top of the newspaper. "Don't do anything I wouldn't do," he quipped.

Jack just smiled as he collected the keys to Sandy's Ford. "Where's Mom?"

"Sleeping in. She tossed and turned most of the night, worrying about Flo, got up and made the cinnamon buns and finally fell asleep. We're on our own, Jackie. Take it easy, whatever you do."

"I will." Jack chewed his lip. "See you later." He grabbed his heavier jacket from a hook by the back door as he left. This early in the morning it could get pretty cold flying.

His heart pounded as he backed the Ford out of the garage. He closed the doors and headed out of town onto the gravel side road. It should take him twenty minutes or so to get to the secondary landing strip at Bushell Park. With any kind of luck Trevor should arrive around the same time, flying a Tiger Moth.

As he pulled up at the airfield, he watched a lone Tiger Moth circle low overhead, then line up above the runway to land. Trevor brought the plane in with hardly a bounce or a bump. Jack strolled out to meet him.

The small plane taxied to a stop. "Hop on up here." Trevor said, grinning. He was wearing his sporty white scarf and his full flying suit, helmet and gear. "Did you bundle up? It will be cold up there."

Jack nodded and clambered into the student cockpit. "Let's go."

Seconds later the Moth taxied down the isolated field and took off into a clear, china-blue sky. This is the life, thought Jack, looking down at the fields and farms as they sailed over them. The little plane wobbled and dipped but some day small planes would be much safer if Jack had his way. They spent the next hour doing loops and spins and taking turns flying the perky little plane.

"You're pretty good for an amateur," Trevor shouted after he had given Jack the controls the first time.

"Thanks. You're not bad yourself."

"Too bad you'll never see me flying a fighter plane."

"You'd like that, wouldn't you – flying a fighter."

"It would be wizard," Trevor said.

Jack spent the next few minutes concentrating on flying the plane.

"You haven't lost your touch," shouted Trevor over the Gosport. "I bet you miss it." Jack grinned at the praise.

Finally it was time to land and Trevor touched down smooth as a skate on ice. With a Tiger Moth that was a challenge.

"Of course I miss flying," said Jack.

"Maybe we can do this again."

"I better get back home. I told Dad I'd wash and wax Sandy's car. Mom is stewing about Flo."

"I hear she's been injured. Basil told me."

"Who on earth would bomb a hospital? Nobody's safe over there."

"I know, and I'm heading home soon. I figure life is short. I'm going to live in the moment. It may be all we have. And at least I get to fly. I'll love it even if it's the last thing I do."

"I hope it won't be."

"You're a good bloke, Jackie."

"We're really different, though. You're a city slicker, a musician, and a flyer. I'm still in school."

"That's why we're such good mates. We don't have to compete, we can just be friends. You remind me of my younger brother, you know. He and I are great mates. My brother Tom is a loner. Maybe it's because of his legs being bad."

Jack nodded. "Some of us are going over to the Hobbs farm for a swim later. Are you and Basil coming?" Jack asked.

"Basil is, for sure. I'll take this crate back and refill the gas tank. I want to write in the next page of my pilot's log."

"You're an eager beaver. That's what my grandpa called me when they let me skip Grade Four," laughed Jack.

"So you're hardly one to talk, are you, Jackie boy? I'll fly over and wave, kiddo."

"Take it easy, Trevor."

"You worry too much."

CHAPTER 22

Later that afternoon Basil, Dexter, Buddy and Jack headed out to the Hobbses' swimming hole. They had their swim trunks on. No skinny-dipping today. Violet and Rose Hobbs had warned the boys they were planning on a dip after they'd practiced with Cathy and Ivy at the church.

You couldn't see the pond from the road. It was surrounded by a windbreak of mixed willow, small birch, poplar trees and wild brush. The track from the farmhouse to the water was well worn and rutted. Jack remembered flying over the farm early in the spring, watching the wandering course of the creek and spotting the pond glinting in the sunlight. He had pointed it out to Sandy.

Now he stretched out on one of his mom's old towels on the grassy slope that led down to the muddy shoreline. You could wade into the cool water or dive off the wooden dock the Hobbs twins had built. On the other side, close to the dam, a family of ducks patrolled. A frog chorus provided the musical entertainment. The frogs were accompanied by flies, bees, dragonflies and other insects. Cattails and lily pads edged the area where the smaller stream wandered on.

Jack turned over to toast his pale back. Basil and Dexter were yelling and throwing water at each other, with Buddy barking happily on the shore, but Jack just felt like loafing.

What a week lay ahead. It made Jack jumpy as a gopher in a hayfield full of foxes. Tonight there was a flying school party. Jack hoped he wouldn't have to dance. He loved big band music by Jimmy Dorsey and Glenn Miller but he had two left feet when it came to the two-step.

Wes came bumping across the grass on his bicycle. He had on baggy swim trunks. "I finished my chores so I thought I'd join you guys." He tossed his bike down and pulled off his T-shirt, slipped out of his running shoes and ran for the water.

Jack sat up, put his arms around his knees and watched his friend slice through the water. Wes was a far better swimmer than Jack. He'd join him in a minute but right now he was going over his agenda in his head. He liked to know what was coming up. It gave Jack some sense of having control of things. He chuckled. He was probably more like his mother than he wanted to admit.

Coming up next Thursday was the dress rehearsal for the fête. Saturday was the performance in the United Church basement. Sunday evening they were performing in Mortlach – taking the show on the road he had laughingly told his parents – and Monday was graduation day at the airfield. It was going to be wild. Life couldn't be any better.

School started a week Tuesday. The RAF boys were slated to leave Wednesday. Life would get back to normal – when? A new bunch of flyers was due a few days after this batch left. But Wes and Jack would be too busy with grade twelve to work at the base, even on the weekends. They both needed scholarships or bursaries or really good part-time jobs. Neither set of parents had money to spare.

Meanwhile he was intent on having a great time now, as Trevor had suggested. He swam out and joined Wes and Dexter in a game of ball. Basil and Buddy were playing in the shallows.

Jack headed back to shore to see his dog. What was he going to do about Buddy when these guys left? That was a problem he hadn't considered yet.

Buddy padded into the water to greet Jack as he emerged from the pond. Basil joined Jack and the dog and hummed tunes from the show as they waited for the girls.

Buddy stretched out on the grass and chewed on a worn bit of rope that he hauled everywhere.

"I'm sure going to miss you guys." Jack sucked on a blade of sweet grass.

"The feeling's mutual, Jack."

"Maybe after the war…"

Basil pulled a green shoot from a stalk of grass and chewed too. "I hope the CO will approve of me getting married before I leave. I want Dr. McLeod to perform the ceremony. I want Cathy to move to England as soon as the war ends."

Jack didn't like the sound of that.

"Trevor thinks we can start a production company to do musical theatre after the war. I'm not sure. I might be better as a lawyer at the bar."

"I can't imagine you in a courtroom," laughed Wes who had come out of the water dripping and shaking water over Jack and Basil.

"My dad sure can. He has his heart set on it. Any news from the front?"

"Not yet." Hovering over every conversation, every event, was a shadow, the cloud called war.

Cathy and the other girls came over the hill, waving towels and laughing together about something. Jack's insides flipped. He leapt up and raced into the pond, dove and came up spluttering. Rose and Violet stood at the edge chattering about how cold it was and how they didn't want to get their hair wet. They both had on swimsuits that showed off their tanned legs. Jack tried not to stare at them.

Buddy came swimming out to Jack with a thick stick. Jack threw it. Buddy fetched it and swam to shore and shook his wet coat all over the girls.

"Call off your dog, boys," laughed Cathy. "We don't want our perfect day ruined."

It was truly a beautiful late summer day. Jack floated on his back, looking up at the endless blue sky, the colour of his mother's fancy Wedgwood teapot. Only a few planes crossed his field of vision. The buzzing of the bees seemed louder than the drone of the small yellow planes.

What a summer he'd had! He glanced over and saw his dog, sitting with his ears up, quivering attentively, his eyes scanning the area around him. Buddy was ready for anything. His old friend Wes was talking to Rose Hobbs. He chuckled, seeing Wes talking to a girl, trying to act like a smooth operator instead of the studious type. It wasn't just the village that had changed with the presence of all these young airmen. He and Wes had changed too.

What was going to happen to Buddy when these flyers left, and what was going to happen to him? Like the string of ducklings following their parents to the next slough and practicing for their flight south, he was perched on the edge of his future. It lay before him, a challenge or a problem, depending on how he tackled it. He had to make plans. He knew he didn't want to back into life, or fall into it, take the easy way.

He wasn't like Trevor, who said he lived for the moment and the day. Jack wanted to move forward, discover his centre of gravity and choose his own course. Follow his dream. He wanted to keep a sense of equilibrium.

Seemingly out of nowhere, a line of dark clouds skidded across the sky from the north and covered the sun. A sharp wind stirred the water and the leaves of the poplars around the swimming hole. Jack swam to shore, where Buddy stood to welcome him, his plumed tail like a gorgeous black feather.

Cathy and the other girls were washing their hair and laughing on the other side of the pond. Basil, Dexter and Wes tossed a beach ball back and forth.

The whine of a small plane approaching caught Jack's attention. He looked up, shielding his eyes. One bright yellow Tiger Moth, 3404, made a pass over the farm.

"It's Trevor!" shouted Jack. "He said he might fly over to say 'hi.'"

The small plane disappeared behind the trees. The buzz faded. Everyone had clambered out of the pond and stood dripping, teeth chattering. Cathy stood, holding Basil's hand.

Trevor reappeared higher up. He rolled and dived, showing off the little plane and his skills. Buddy sat close to Jack, still as a rock, his eyes following the plane in its flight. The dog growled deep in his throat.

"It's okay, Buddy. It's just Trevor showing his stuff."

Jack had a crick in his neck but he didn't dare look down. He didn't want to miss the show. Trevor flew high, low, and rolled and dived in the little kite. Jack shivered as a stray wind blew across the pond. Dark shadows of an eagle being chased by two screaming crows crossed his line of vision and then disappeared in the distance.

Everyone at the swimming hole had stopped to watch.

Jack was entranced. He loved watching the hard-working biplane manoeuvre. How many young flyers had flown these training planes? A Tiger Moth was not elegant but she was tight and tidy, like a small but sturdy hockey player on a frozen slough.

Jack longed to be up there with his friend.

Buddy started barking – as if he knew his good friend Trevor was in the plane overhead. Jack shook his head. "He can't hear you, Buddy, not above the noise of the engine."

Buddy bounded up and down the shore of the pond, barking furiously.

"Don't worry, Buddy. He'll head back to base soon."

Trevor came in low for another sweep over the pond. He waved as he passed, then climbed sharply out of sight.

The engine sputtered. Jack heard a loud pop, and a raucous bang. Then a silence that went on too long. Only the whine of wind and hum of insects filled the air. It was not enough. What had happened to Trevor and the Tiger Moth?

Jack stopped breathing. His ears plugged as if he was diving too deep, too fast. His skull hurt as if it was being compressed under tons of water. He was drowning.

Crash! Whoosh! The crackle of flames and the sighing of the wind.

Clouds of smoke and dust rose from Hobbs' hayfield. Buddy ran like lightning. Basil, Dexter, Wes and Jack raced, bare feet on stubble, avoiding stooks of drying alfalfa, across the field to the creek bed where the yellow Moth lay crumpled and burning. It was a total wreck. No one could see through the haze and scattered debris. Jack shook like a leaf. There was nothing or no one to see. He knew that like he knew his own name.

Buddy had beaten them all to the site. He pawed the scorched and blackened earth.

The stench of gasoline was everywhere. The girls arrived, shivering. Cathy ran toward the burnt-out plane but stopped.

"Stay back!" Basil pulled her close.

"Trevor!" Cathy began to shake.

The young people huddled in a semicircle.

"He's gone," said Basil.

"Someone go for help!" Jack yelled.

Crash! The shriek of a second explosion echoed across the open prairie.

"It's the gas tank!" shouted Basil.

Rose and Violet ran to the farmhouse. Dexter raced to phone the base. Jack stood in shock by Wes.

Cathy dropped to the ground with Basil holding her in his arms. She rocked and cried, rocked and cried. "No! God, no!"

Buddy stayed a safe distance from the smouldering wreckage, whining. He sat unmoving, like a sentinel, Trevor's white scarf caught under his paw, scorched, tattered, grimy but intact.

The dog's whiskers were singed. Jack sat down beside him He hugged the trembling pup. "You're a good dog," he said.

Jack walked back to the pond in a kind of daze, the dog padding slowly beside him.

His mouth was dry as a desert, his tongue thick. Nothing, but nothing, would ever be the same.

Only this morning he had been in this plane with Trevor. They did the same manoeuvres. He'd been flying the Moth for some of them. And now the Moth and Trevor were gone. And he, Jack Waters, was alive and safe on the ground. Life was not fair.

He dove into the pond and swam across it and back, wanting to get away, far away, from the scene in the field. His tears mingled with the water. He dove to the bottom of the pond and tried to stay down. When his lungs were about to burst, he rose to the surface, gasping for air.

He heard sounds of a motorcycle, a truck and an ambulance racing toward them. He ran with the others to meet them – to describe the crash and the death of Trevor Knight, the sudden, horrible death of a seventeen-year-old who had flown into everyone's hearts in Cairn, Saskatchewan, in 1943.

He was my brother, thought Jack, and now he's gone.

CHAPTER 23

asil ran around at the Thursday night dress rehearsal with his clipboard and lists, and the crowd of performers and stagehands followed his directions. Jack was the gopher – go-fer this and go-fer that. People moved either like molasses in January or like a flock of wild ducks, depending on their moods.

The whole hall rang with song, dance, shouted directions and people being alternately hushed and encouraged to sing up, speak up, or hurry up and get on stage quickly and off quietly. The smell of weak coffee and strong tea permeated the room. Repete Nelson, without even waiting for a sign from Jimmy, helped by climbing ladders and stringing streamers and balloons.

Buddy sat under Basil's chair guarding his uniform jacket and supplies, keeping a sharp lookout for his remaining family. Now, except for Jack, Basil seemed to be Buddy's favourite. Buddy would be sad when Basil and Dexter left.

Jack sang along with Basil in his Gilbert and Sullivan parody. He hummed through the station band's medley of tunes. Then his turn came, first with the church choir, then the quartet with Wes and Basil, and Cathy replacing Trevor. He struggled with tears singing the tenor line – I'll remember you always. Cathy sang Trevor's part in "Always" beside him, her voice true as a tuning fork. Finally the men's chorus took their turn. Arnie Hobbs and Howie Wong stood in the front row of the group belting out the tunes. He was glad the old guys were having fun.

For the finale, the whole cast lined up on stage, more than twenty-five of them, leaving only a handful of spectators. Afterwards, Basil addressed them.

"At ease, everyone," said Basil. "It went well. Just a few pointers." He proceeded to outline where each act needed work. Jack admired the young flyer's finesse in handling such a wide variety of talent and effort. Especially now that he was doing it without Trevor. He probably *would* make a good lawyer. His dad would be proud.

Basil did just about everything well. Cathy beamed at her fiancé.

"I want to tell you how much I appreciate all the work you've put into this production. Trevor would have been pleased."

There was a hush in the room. Jack had to look away, his eyes clouding with tears again. He was finding out first-hand what grief felt like.

"I must admit, "Basil went on, "that when I first arrived in Cairn I thought I had come to the end of the world. But your hospitality and team spirit, and your talent and hard work as we have prepared this show, have made me change my mind about 'colonials.'" A few people smiled.

"If I didn't have a brilliant future in my dad's law firm or on the British stage," here everyone laughed and clapped at his attempt at humour, "I'd contemplate staying in Canada. Of course, I am planning on sending for a grand souvenir, a beautiful Canadian woman, who will join me after the war." More laughter.

"Thank you all for your able assistance. Now I suggest you go home, have a good sleep and take the day off tomorrow. We've got a show to put on."

Suddenly Jack found himself on his feet. "How about a hip-hip-hurray for Basil, for putting us through our paces."

Basil blushed. "If it hadn't been for Trevor Knight, none of this would have happened," he said. "Our performances this weekend will honour his memory."

The hall resounded with thirty or so voices shouting together. They sang hurrah for Trevor and then for Basil. Everyone clapped and began gathering up their stuff.

"What do you think, Jack?" Basil asked as he closed the church door. "Would Trevor be pleased?"

"It'll be wizard." That was the word Trevor would've used, Jack thought.

"See you Saturday, lads and lassies! Break a leg," Basil called to the groups of performers as they strolled away. He and Cathy were headed over to her house. They had to make plans. It didn't look as if the RAF were going to let Basil get married before he left for England.

Wes and Jack piled into the old truck. Dexter and some of the other singers from the aerodrome climbed in the box at the back. Dexter and Basil had gone back to Moose Jaw a couple of weeks ago for the jalopy but it had disappeared. Now everyone relied on Jack to drive them in his dad's truck. He was reluctant to use Sandy's car. He didn't want anything to happen to it.

He drove the singers out to the airport canteen, and they sang silly songs all the way. It was difficult, carrying on after the crash. But most people hadn't known Trevor the way Jack had.

The whole gang – Basil, Dexter, Wes, Cathy and Jack – had taken the British "stiff upper lip" to new heights. When

Jack was alone, however, grief swept over him like a snow-storm in February.

He hadn't been able to sleep all week. He kept talking to Trevor, trying to bring him back in his mind. Each morning he woke lonelier than the day before, more clear that his good mate had gone forever. "You're better living in the moment, Jackie," Trevor had said. It was not an easy thing to learn.

After they'd let the group off at the canteen, Jack and Wes headed back to town.

"How's it really going, Jack?" Wes studied Jack's face. "You miss Trevor lots."

Jack gulped. He wasn't sure he could trust himself to talk about the accident.

"This isn't easy," said Wes. "I guess friends dying never is."

"It's not fair. Some old lady at church told me it was God's will. I don't believe that."

"I don't think life is fair. And I don't think Trevor's death was God's will." Wes chewed his lip.

"You don't?"

"No. I've been doing a lot of thinking this summer," said Wes. "You know, about what I want to do, what my dad wants me to do, what life is really about, what God is like. You've been busy working, hanging out with Basil, Trevor and the gang in your spare time, making models and stewing about technical stuff."

"We've been on different wavelengths, you might say," Jack mused. "What's this got to do with Trevor's death?"

"I'm getting to that." Wes wiped the dust off the dashboard with his left hand.

"I think this war will teach us a lot of lessons, lessons about the human condition." Rain streamed down the window. A lightning bolt lit up the sky in the east.

Jack turned the windshield wipers on. "So?"

"So I don't think we understand God anymore, not like we used to think we did. God is not in charge of the war, of who dies, or who doesn't, or who wins. I think we've got a lot to explain to God. We need to take responsibility for our own actions. Trevor died. It was an accident. It wasn't God's fault. We need to celebrate his life and the gifts he offered."

"He told me he lived in the moment." Jack could feel his throat tighten. "He said he didn't mind dying if he'd be flying. But I thought it would be in the war."

"I think we honour that, Jackie. We remember all the good times we had together and we get on with our lives." Wes turned and looked closely at Jack.

Jack sighed. "It's hard to figure out how to do that."

"I've been thinking I'd like to study for the ministry. My dad has always hoped I'd follow in his footsteps. That's not why I'm doing it, though. I want to figure out what God really looks like, what Jesus really said, and how in heck we human beings can learn to live together on this earth without killing each other."

"I thought you were going to be a writer?"

"Maybe I could write about it." Wes grinned. "After I've got something worth writing about."

Jack didn't say anything for a moment. As he pulled into the village and slowed to a stop in front of McLeod's house, he said. "I'll fix the technical problems and you fix the spiritual ones. Hey, Wes, it sounds like a great plan."

"I was afraid you'd think I was an idiot, some kind of religious freak."

"Just don't start preaching at me."

"No, sir!"

On Friday morning, as Jack was checking the tires on 3828, Harold hollered from the office door. He was holding the phone in his hand and motioned Jack to hurry.

Jack sprinted across the hangar to the glassed-in area, politely called the office, but really a hodgepodge of an old desk, a typewriter, a couple of rickety chairs and an assortment of unfiled documents, logbooks, mechanical drawings and dingy coffee and tea cups.

"It's your mother, Jack." Harold stood in the doorway holding the receiver out to him.

Jack's heart beat fast and a wave of fear threatened to overpower him. He took the receiver.

"I don't care who hears this, Jack. We've had a letter from Flo. She's better. She's somewhere in England on leave. It's taken a few weeks but she's really on the mend. She's got lots of stories, she says, to tell you and Dad."

"That's great, Mom." Jack had a sudden image of Flo smiling at him from across the room.

"I thought you'd want to know. Here's your dad."

"Jack, I thought you'd like to know she had to be flown to the hospital she's been recovering in."

"You think she was in a field hospital when she got hit?"

"Sounds like it to me, sport. She's one spunky gal, our Flo."

"See you later, Dad."

"Don't work too hard."

Jack said goodbye and handed the phone back to Harold.

"What's up?" Harold asked.

Jack flopped down on one of the rickety chairs. "My sister's all right. She's safe. She's getting better." He wanted to race the length of the hangar and back and scream at the top of his lungs. But he didn't. He just told the rest of the guys the news.

By now the whole of Cairn would know, if anyone on the party line had been listening to their family conversation.

Just then, a bunch of flyers arrived wanting to go up and the ground crew scurried to get the planes ready to fly.

Harold sent him home.

He grabbed his bike and cycled back to Cairn.

His mom and dad were drinking tea and chatting. They stopped and welcomed him with open arms. The Waters family was not a huggy family but this was a special occasion.

"Jack, we've been talking," his dad said. "Ever since we heard the news about Flo."

We've been thinking about our future," his mother said. "We've been thinking about moving, moving to wherever you go to university, especially if your dad can find a job."

"What about the store?" Jack asked.

"Running the store is out of the question," his mother said. "Your dad's sciatica is a chronic condition."

"Unless you want to stay in Cairn…" Dad said.

"Running the family store has never been in my plans."

"This village doesn't need two general stores," his mother said. "I'd like to try and get a job teaching piano, and playing organ in a city church." Playing with Basil and Trevor must have given Jack's mother renewed confidence in her ability.

"I really want to go back on the road," Bill had said. "See a new territory."

Jack wondered if that was such a great idea. Wouldn't that be as hard on his back as running a store? But then again, his dad liked being on the road.

Jack got dizzy thinking of the changes that lay ahead.

CHAPTER 24

veryone in town came to the performance on Saturday night, but the audience was subdued. People whispered instead of their normal chatter. Yesterday there had been a short formal funeral service for Trevor at the flying school but most of the village hadn't been there. This was the first chance for Trevor's friends in Cairn to gather.

Dr. McLeod dedicated the concert to Trevor's memory.

"Trevor was a wonderful young chap with more talent in his little finger than most of us have in our whole being. Just knowing him for the few months he was here was a treat. I can't believe he's gone. None of us can."

Jack blinked to keep tears from falling. He looked over at his mother, sitting at the piano. Her back was ramrod straight, her hands ready in her lap to play "God Save the King" and "O Canada." She really must have been a

Chautauqua girl. The show would go on and she'd play even though Trevor, one of her favourite student pilots ever, was gone.

At least she didn't have to worry about Flo now.

"I'll always think of Trevor soaring," continued Dr. McLeod. "Whether it was in song or in a plane, he reached for the highest and the best. He set us quite a standard. We'll miss him. Besides that, he was a gentle lad who made lots of friends both in the village and on the base."

Jack grinned behind his hand. How little Dr. McLeod understood Trevor's other side. Jack remembered the not-so-gentle way Trevor had reacted when he was attacked on the street in Moose Jaw.

Jack figured they survived the performance on sheer nerve. It went pretty smoothly except for the usual screw-ups. Dexter's cards fell on the floor, the Boyles' fiddler knocked over her music stand, and Jack couldn't sing worth a bean. But Arnie carried the tenors in style.

The Boyles amazed the whole village and maybe even themselves. Jerry Boyle and his oldest daughter and Jimmy stood together at the front of the stage with the younger Boyles in the back row. Obviously the older ones were the better dancers. The fiddle player from Mortlach played a series of jigs and reels and the Boyles, wearing first tap shoes and then changing to black fitted dance shoes, strutted their stuff. The old man was huffing and puffing by the end, but the audience clapped so hard the Boyles performed an encore. Jimmy grinned at the audience as the Boyles finished their final twirl. They bowed and danced off.

Jack felt a strange moment of pride in his old enemy. Who would have guessed Jimmy and his family had all that talent? If Trevor and Basil hadn't dreamt up this fête, no one in the village would ever have known. As Jimmy passed Jack on his way back to his seat, Jack leaned out into the aisle.

"Great job, Jimmy."

Jimmy stopped and turned to acknowledge Jack. He grinned. "All in a day's work, Jackie." Then he sauntered on.

It was the happiest Jack had ever seen Jimmy Boyle.

Everyone had wondered whether Cathy would still sing her solo. Trevor had been her accompanist and a good friend to both her and Basil. "I can do it," she'd said, "if Mrs. Waters will play for me." She stood, tall and willowy, her hair braided. Wearing her "Dorothy" dress, she cupped her hands as if holding a bunch of flowers in front of her and sang in a clear, strong voice, tears streaming down her face.

The song was familiar to everyone who'd seen Judy Garland in *The Wizard of Oz*, one of the first Technicolor movies ever made. Jack had only been nine when it came out. "Somewhere Over the Rainbow" seemed like just the right song for Cathy to sing for Trevor. It talked about blue skies and dreams coming true and bluebirds flying over the rainbow and how she, the singer, could fly too.

There was something about music. It had real staying power. Jack had grown up listening to his mother playing everything from pop tunes to Bach. A melody played well lifted the spirit of a person the same way a well-tuned airplane lifted a pilot. And after the sound died away the melody played on inside your head. For a moment Jack allowed himself to soar with Cathy's voice and forget the war, the grief and the worry of being Jack Waters.

As Ivy played the last chords, there was a moment's silence. Cathy curtseyed. Jack stood and applauded. Around him chairs scraped on the floor as others stood and joined with him. Some villagers sobbed, some had tears on their cheeks and some just clapped. Were they clapping for Cathy or Trevor, or both? The applause filled the room and overflowed into the empty streets beyond.

Did the notes of Cathy's song float out the windows, join with the din of crickets and frogs and become part of the deep Saskatchewan night? Jack knew he would always remember this night, this concert and this song.

How Jack wished Trevor could be here. Who knew, maybe he was. Maybe summer and life had not died in that farmer's field. For Jack, it might be the end of summer holidays, but there was still a lot to do. Get this bunch of RAF pilots sent off, especially Basil, hope for news of Sandy, get ready for grade twelve, figure out what to do with Buddy.

Everyone laughed at Basil's song, "The Pilots of the Prairies," which gave new words to a famous song from a Gilbert and Sullivan operetta. Basil's voice was clear and loud as he talked about how a talent for singing and an attention to detail were the keys to doing well in the air force. For a moment he seemed to bring the glamour of the London stage to the small prairie village, and when he reached the final chorus, "Keep your feet on the ground, stay out of the blue/ And you'll all make Marshals of the King's Air Crew" – he brought the house down.

After the concert Buddy got in the back of the truck and wouldn't budge. His fur was still singed around his muzzle and the tips of his ears from the crash last weekend. He whined mournfully. Jack shook his head.

It was nearly eleven o'clock when Jack got home after driving Dexter and some of the other flyers back to the flying school. The dog was still in the back of the truck. He had refused to get out at the H-hut even though Dexter had tried to coax him with a bone.

Jack's mom and dad were sitting in the backyard on the canvas deck chairs. Ivy was dabbing her eyes with a lace handkerchief. In the light cast by the lamp above the back door, Bill was working on a small table, rolling dimes from the cash register into papers for the bank.

"Is something wrong?" Jack asked, panic hitting his stomach and making it tighter than a drumhead. "Is there news about Sandy?"

"No, Jack, it's not that," said Ivy. "It's…"

"Jackie." His dad cleared his throat. "Your mother and I couldn't sleep…"

Jack sensed rather than heard Buddy come up beside him. The dog must have jumped out of the truck. Buddy sat quietly beside him.

"Maybe it's hearing Flo is going to be all right or…" His mother started a sentence and stopped. "I keep thinking about Trevor. He was such a fine boy. I've been wondering about how his family feels, his mom and brothers especially…"

"It's been too much lately," Dad said. "But we'll manage, Ivy. Can I make you some tea?"

"I'm all right, Bill," Mom said. "The fête was a lot of work and Trevor would have loved it. He was a good musician." She shuddered even though the evening air was balmy and the night sky glorious. "He sure loved that dog you found."

"He did love Buddy," said Jack.

The dog heard his name. He left Jack's side and padded over to where Ivy Waters was sitting, one hand holding the wooden armrest while the other one clasped the hankie in her lap. The dog sat politely, then calmly rested his muzzle on her lap, his big brown eyes gazing wistfully at Ivy's sorrowing face. Jack didn't dare move. It was as if the dog sensed Ivy's pain and maybe some of his own, missing the cheerful presence of Trevor Knight.

There was a moment or two of silence. His mother gazed down at the dog. She didn't move.

"Speaking of Buddy," Dad said, "Mom and I were discussing what would become of him once Basil and Dexter left. He won't know the new students. He's gotten attached to the boys who are leaving."

Jack hadn't breathed deeply since Buddy had gone to his mother. She was studying the dog as if seeing him for the first time. "He seems friendly. He's calmed down a lot," his mother said.

Jack dared to glance over at his dad, his good old persistent dad. He hadn't forgotten about Jack and his dog.

"I've been training him in my spare time at work. But I won't be at the maintenance shop anymore."

"That's what I told Ivy." His dad placed the rolled-up coins in a shoebox.

"Trevor would want the dog to have a real home," said Mom. "He loved dogs."

"So do I, Mom, so do I!"

Ivy patted the dog's head, then stood up, gently brushing Buddy aside. She wiped her hands on her damp hankie.

"Trevor's gone," she said. "Buddy belongs with you now. You better build him a doghouse, though. He can come in when it's really cold in the winter."

Jack didn't know what to say. He stared at his mother. Her eyes were red from crying, the fancy hankie wadded in her hand.

"Buddy has a doghouse at the base," said Jack. "Cheese built it for him. I'll fetch it."

"Trevor is buried in the cemetery close to your Uncle Jack. It seems fitting that the dog come to us." His mother was talking but she wasn't looking at him. She was staring into space.

"Two talented young men who were both casualties of war, one who crashed with his dreams intact, and one who lost his dreams in the sky over Europe. We will mourn them both."

"Mom, are you sure about Buddy?" Jack asked.

"No, Jackie. Frankly I'm not. I'm not sure about anything. But that isn't what's important right now." His mother folded the damp, crumpled hankie neatly and put it on the small table beside the shoebox filled with rolled coins. She spoke slowly and with great effort.

"I thought I could keep you safe, keep life simple, Jackie, keep you young and innocent. I didn't want you to feel grief like I've felt."

"Then the war started," his dad said.

"The flying school was built," added his mother. "Flo and Sandy left."

"Cairn changed." Dad cleared his throat.

"The flyers came," said Jack. "Trevor came."

"He was going to be the best man at Cathy and Basil's wedding," Mom said.

His dad chuckled. "I don't know what changed us most – the arrival of the British Commonwealth Air Training Plan, Flo leaving home and being hurt or Sandy going missing in action. But the Waters family will never be the same."

"Enough of this." Jack's mom smoothed the wrinkles on her navy dress. "Where are you going to put that dog for the night?"

"I'll tie him out here in the yard. Tomorrow afternoon I'll bring the doghouse home."

Dad carried the chairs into the back shed and took the shoebox and Mom's hankie into the house. He grinned at Jack before he disappeared into the house.

"Thanks, Dad." Jack figured his dad had put in a good word for Buddy before Jack had gotten home. He was pretty clever for an old guy.

"Get some sleep, Jack," his mother said. "We've got another performance tomorrow and Basil's graduation is Monday. And don't forget school starts on Tuesday."

"The Grade Twelves don't have to show up until Wednesday."

"Did you know Trevor was only seventeen, Jack?"

"I figured it out. He was talking about his older brother Tom who was eighteen and I asked him if they were twins. He got all embarrassed and I realized he'd used his brother's birth certificate to sign up. He doctored the Thomas to look like Trevor instead."

"I'm glad you're only sixteen. Thank goodness your dad was too young for the Great War and too old for the Second World War." His mother headed toward the door.

"Don't stay out long. Just settle Buddy and get to bed."

"I'm pretty keyed up after tonight's performance. I'm going for a walk." Then Jack added. "Thanks for letting me keep Buddy, Mom. You won't regret it."

"Don't stay out too long. Have you a sweater on? It's chilly."

Jack smiled to himself. *Some* things never changed.

CHAPTER 25

On Tuesday, Wes and Jack stood out on the prairie, beside their bikes, watching the planes in the distance landing and taking off. They were taking advantage of their last free weekday to take a long ride. They had lunches in their carriers – and thanks to Ivy's coaxing – sweaters in case the weather changed.

Watching planes was more fun than watching geese or ducks in the spring and fall, the way they had when they were small.

The war had changed the skies over Cairn. In fact, it had probably changed the skies everywhere. Jack had a feeling that airplanes were here to stay and he'd be watching them for years to come. He might even be flying one of his own someday.

When Jack and Wes weren't watching, they were listening to the buzz of aircraft, louder than a swarm of bees. By now they could differentiate one model from another and Jack could tell what shape the engine was in. Each had a language all its own.

A Tiger Moth was flying overhead when suddenly the engine stuttered, misfired and the small plane descended slowly with obviously reduced power, moving west in the direction of Mortlach.

"Oh, no! Not another one," shouted Wes.

"Looks like he's trying to land." Jack listened for a crash but none came. "It's just a forced landing, Wes, not a crash! Let's see if we can help!"

No one could have saved Trevor. But Jack had to make sure this pilot was all right. It was a lousy landing, not a crash. Jack knew how to deal with the small problems. Working with Harold and Angus had taught him that.

The boys headed in the direction of the downed plane.

The Boyles' old pickup came toward them, raising dust clouds and scattering pea gravel. "Some idiot's pranged in a farmer's field back there," old man Boyle yelled as he passed them.

"Was he all right?" Jack hollered, but Boyle was too far away.

Wes pedalled steadily, beads of sweat streaming down his red face – or were they tears? He stood high like a jockey on a thoroughbred racehorse. "God, not another one!"

Wes didn't swear. Jack knew that. He was praying out loud as he pedalled furiously down the Mortlach road.

Jack kept pace with him. "It's going to be fine, Wes. He's probably sitting there trying to figure out how to get back to the airfield." He hoped he was right. A pilot could get hurt going down on a rough field. He hoped old man Boyle would call the aerodrome.

As they came over a slight rise in the road, miles from any houses, they spotted the plane. She was sitting in a pasture, her left wings tipped down and the tire on the left side stuck in a gaping hole. She was 3828, Basil's favourite plane.

Jack dropped his bike and sprinted across the ditch and a small creek, and scooted under the fence where Wes held up the wire for him. The two of them raced to the Moth and Wes, being taller, leaned over the wing to check the cockpit.

It was smattered with blood and feathers, a real mess. It took the two of them to pull the Perspex back because it was damaged. "Is that blood?" asked Wes.

"It looks like duck or goose, what with all those feathers clinging to the windscreen. Who is it anyway?"

"It's Basil. He's out cold."

"See if you can wake him up, Wes."

Jack moved to the front of the plane and stared at the cowling on the engine and the propeller while Wes bent over the crumpled form of Basil.

"I wish he'd wake up." Wes touched Basil's shoulder, reached in and undid the helmet and loosened his flying jacket and scarf at the neck. "His skin is warm."

"The engine isn't smoking or anything." Jack was all business. "There's a bunch of gunk in it. The propeller is all right. There's a gash in the fabric on the right wing, not enough to ground it. How's Basil?"

"He's not good." Wes stood helpless. "What can we do?"

Jack joined Wes. His breath caught in his throat. Basil's helmet slid sideways, revealing a great gash on their friend's forehead and blood seeping into the blond hair. A vein in Basil's throat pulsed. Thank God he was alive. But he was unconscious and still bleeding.

Jack took a big breath. Basil was in rough shape. Cathy didn't need anything really bad to happen to her fiancé. Not if Jack could help. None of them needed any more unhappy endings. What could Jack do? That was the question.

Wes's face was ashen. A shock of reddish hair fell over his eyes. He gulped. "How bad is it?"

"He needs a doctor."

"Should we get him out?" Wes stared into the cockpit.

"I'd be afraid to move him. He's probably got a concussion. Maybe there's something broken."

"I could cycle back to the Hobbs place." Wes turned as if anxious to go.

"It's too far. The longer a person's unconscious, the worse it is."

"I could go for help to the base."

"Basil, Basil, wake up!" Jack hollered. "It's at least ten miles to the airbase by road, Wes." He rejoined Wes by the wing. "It would take too long."

"I could cycle to the closest farm or on to Mortlach."

"Can you stop the bleeding with your hankie?" A daring thought edged its way into Jack's consciousness. "We don't know how long he'll be unconscious." Jack's head felt clogged and his ears were ringing. He could smell his own sweat. "We don't know whether he has other injuries."

Could he get this crate flying again and take Basil back to base?

"It's only ten minutes to the airfield by plane."

"But Basil's unconscious. The plane's damaged," said Wes.

"I can fly a plane," Jack said. "We can patch the plane up fast."

Jack stared around the field as if looking for advice from someone wiser than himself. He spotted an old shed across the gravel road. "Go check out that shed. See if the farmer has left stuff there. Maybe some machine oil or a few pails or cans to fetch water in."

His heart beat so loudly he was surprised it didn't drown out his voice. He had his left hand on Basil's shoulder. The soft well-worn leather of the flight jacket felt like a second skin. "Basil, wake up, please."

"Jack, what are you thinking?" Wes looked sick.

" If he woke up, I could fly with him, make sure he was all right."

Wes stared at the front of the plane. "But the cowling is full of bird parts."

"We can fix that pretty fast."

The poor dumb bird had flown right into the propeller. Jack started pulling chunks of bloody muscle, tissue and bone off the cowling.

"Yuk!" Wes stepped back.

"The one I fixed wasn't quite as bad as this. Dexter landed it safely on the end of the strip. We hauled it in. We repaired it. A bucket of water and one of lubricating oil would help." Jack went to work.

Wes ran to the nearby creek and brought his cap back full of fresh water. Jack used his white hankie to clear away the mess and kept working on the engine. Wes ran across the road to the old shed and carried a tin can of oil from a drum. Then he fetched a can full of water from the creek. He checked Basil again. "I don't like the looks of the blood running."

"No luck stopping it, Wes?"

"Nope."

"Too bad the doctor hasn't driven by."

"That's a good idea, Jack. Let's go for the doctor."

"Wes, I'm thinking." Jack bent down and stared at the wheels and the field in front of the plane.

"I hope you aren't thinking what I think you're thinking." Wes's eyes were wide as a frightened rabbit's.

"I can't just leave him here. Wes, I know how to fly."

"It's too dangerous."

"Have you got a better idea?"

"It can't be too far to a farmhouse."

"His breathing is shallow. He's bleeding. We don't know if he's got internal injuries."

"But…"

"Wes, think how long it would take for the ambulance from the infirmary to get here. Add that to any ride to a farmhouse and a phone. You're talking about an hour at least. We can have this plane up and out of here in a matter of minutes."

Wes sighed and shook his head.

"Are you going to help me or not?"

Wes looked longingly down the road in both directions as if praying for a vehicle to drive by. The quiet prairie stretched around them. A few frogs sang and a flock of sparrows rose and fluttered in the still air.

"Okay, but I still think it's dangerous."

Jack worked quickly, trying not to think of Trevor's accident – the sharp drop of the biplane, the flames, the black smoke, the explosion. The terrible silence after.

Basil wasn't moving. There were no planes in the sky, no cars on the road. There was only himself and Wes and Basil Skelton, a young RAF pilot who'd just gotten his wings, the guy Cathy was going to marry. Jack's mind raced faster than a car motor. Sandy let me take off once. But I've never landed a plane. I could save Basil's life or I could kill both of us.

Jack's mind flicked to Sandy, missing in action, his sister recovering from her injuries so she could continue nursing wounded or dying soldiers, and Trevor in the cemetery, close to Uncle Jack.

He knew what he had to do.

Wes and Jack, working together, lifted the tire out of the hole so the Tiger Moth could roll forward. Thank goodness it was a light plane.

Jack talked to himself as he removed the last of the bird parts. I promised my mother I wouldn't do anything dangerous. But that was before Trevor died, and he was my best friend in the whole world except for Wes.

"Did you practice landing?" asked Wes, probably guessing the truth when Jack didn't answer.

Jack checked Basil as he climbed in the front section of the cockpit. Basil's shoulder twitched under his hand. Everything looked in good order: the instrument panel, the stick and the pedals. Jack shuddered. Anxiety, fear and doubt knotted in Jack's stomach and his throat turned to iron.

Courage is not a gift; it is a decision. That's what Arnie had said. A young man had to decide what mattered and act.

He jumped down. "Help me roll this bird into the middle of the pasture." Given his lack of experience, Jack knew he would have a better chance of getting the plane into the air if he had a flat surface.

They hauled and then pushed the small plane to the smoothest part of the field. Prairie dust rose in clouds. Wes sneezed. Jack collected himself for one moment then climbed into the forward cockpit.

"Try the propeller, Wes. Give it a whirl or two." Remembering Angus, he added, "Make sure you stand clear when it starts firing."

He fastened his seat belt, checked the dials. The fuel was fine. He sucked one finger and put it into the air. The wind was from the west. He was pointed west. "That's good," he said to himself, thinking of the Station Standing Orders. "Always take off into the wind."

Wes spun the propeller…the engine caught. Wes ran around and closed the canopy. He scrubbed some of the dead bird from the windscreen with Basil's silk scarf so Jack could see out, but it was still pretty messy.

Jack taxied forward slowly, trying to get a feel for the plane. "It's like riding a bicycle," Sandy had told him. "You never forget." What would Sandy have done? Fly the plane. That's what both Sandy and Trevor would have done. Jack was doing the right thing.

The plane bounced and bumped along. Jack put his hand on the stick, feet on the rudder pedals, and thought himself back into the mind of a flyer.

He advanced the throttle, and pulled the Moth's nose up. The engine stuttered and caught, stuttered and caught, with Jack still on the ground moving forward more quickly every moment. Why wasn't the plane lifting? Beads of sweat popped out on his forehead.

He took a deep breath. Jackie Waters was a very cautious, methodical fellow, that's what Harold, his boss at the airfield had said. He was reliable. So he wasn't going to lose his nerve now.

The tires bumped and jarred, the wings tilted first one way and then another. Ahead of him, about a hundred yards away, stood an outcropping of stunted poplar and birch. He had to get the plane in the air before he reached there.

Jack clenched his jaw. His stomach was plastered to his backbone. He ordered his hands to stop shaking, pushed the throttle ahead and headed the nose up. Checked his dials. No time to veer to the left or right. He saw the tangled branches coming closer, imagined the plane tearing into them. He pulled up the nose as hard as he could.

Just yards from the bluff, the Tiger Moth lifted off, wobbling and weaving, its belly touching the top branches. It wasn't a glorious takeoff, but he was in the air. Jack nosed up into the wide sky with a sigh of relief. Now he had to keep the plane on course, straight and steady.

He turned the plane north and then east, back toward Cairn airfield.

The engine sounded a little rough. Good job it wasn't far to the base. The tower appeared on the horizon, straight ahead.

"All aircraft taking off or landing must do so into the wind." That meant he had to fly across the airport and turn to come back into the wind. That would put him on Runway One. He checked his height. "Aircraft are not to be flown across the aerodrome at a height of less than 2,000 feet unless they are landing or taking off."

Jack was flying at 1,000 feet. He wasn't too comfortable heading up higher, but he knew the rules. He nosed up as he headed east. "Any aircraft at a height of less than 6,000 feet will make a left-hand circuit when in the vicinity of the aerodrome." Jack turned north a mile or so beyond the airport and headed down at a proper angle and slowing speed. He gritted his teeth and reminded himself to breathe.

"What's up?" a weak voice came through the Gosport. "Who the heck is flying this plane?"

Jack glanced back into Basil's pasty face. Dried blood spattered his forehead and a thin stream of fresh blood ran down his cheek.

Suddenly Jack's hands shook like aspen leaves and his heart raced. "Basil, are you all right?"

"Not very likely. What happened?"

"You were attacked by a goose. Your engine gave out. Wes and I saw you come down. I pulled most of the goose parts out of the works." Jack gulped. Maybe Basil could land the plane. "I'm not very good at landing."

"I'm feeling pretty crook."

Jack turned and looked back. Basil's head had dropped to the side again. He was out cold.

His hopes dashed, Jack steeled himself to land the plane.

He levelled the Tiger Moth and approached the runway. He bounced and the plane lifted off again. He throttled down, holding the wings as level as he could. His angle of descent was fine. His speed was on target. It was as if the page on landing the plane was inscribed inside his skull. Jack focused his mind. He had no time for any thoughts other than following the procedures for landing a training plane. Moments later the plane was taxiing straight at the hangar, toward two parked Tiger Moths. Jack stopped breathing. He put both feet on the toe brakes and willed the small plane to stop without running into anything. A maintenance truck and a tractor sat to the left. Two Ansons sat to the right.

At the last moment the Tiger Moth stopped, its nose nearly touching the parked planes.

Jack pulled back the canopy, hauled himself out and dropped to the ground. The station ambulance pulled up and a doctor and nurse leapt out. "Are you all right?" the nurse asked Jack. "Boyle phoned to tell us there was a plane down." Jack nodded and shook himself all over. The doctor and ground crew loaded Basil into the ambulance.

Harold and a couple of the other maintenance men came striding out to the plane. "Who in heck landed that plane?" Harold shouted. "He nearly caused an accident."

"Sorry about that!" Jack nearly collapsed when he tried to walk. He was bathed in a cold sweat. Harold and Angus helped him into the hangar. Buddy came bounding over from his favourite spot by the fence where Basil usually parked him.

Angus settled Jack in a chair, offered him water. "You flew the plane," he said with amazement. "A lousy landing though, lad." Buddy curled at Jack's feet.

"But he landed the dang thing!" said Harold. "What's the story?"

Jack sipped water and told them everything, first about his flight today, and then about his lessons with Sandy and Trevor.

"You're a sly one, aren't you, Jackie boy?" said Harold.

A few minutes later Wes came strolling into the hangar. "I phoned Dad from the nearest farm. He came and got me. I had to check that you were all right."

Buddy leapt up on Wes, nearly dumping him over. Someone needed to train this dog to behave better. He was getting too strong for his own good and the good of those who tangled with him. He smelled bad, too. He needed a bath. So did Jack.

"What happened?" asked Wes. "How come the plane is sitting so close to the hangar?"

"I had a hard time landing it." Jack managed a crooked grin.

"What about Basil?"

"They took him to the infirmary. We'll find out soon enough. If it's really bad they'll take him into Moose Jaw."

Buddy was licking Jack's hand, which was sweaty from holding the stick in a state of panic.

"How'd you get here, Buddy? Did Basil pick you up this morning?"

"The dog may be smart," laughed Wes, "but he can't talk."

"I left Buddy tied in the yard, though."

"I think Basil came in to see Cathy off to her first day teaching. He probably wanted a last day with the pup."

"Thanks for helping me, Wes," Jack said. "I couldn't have done it without you." His mind flashed on Wes bringing the water, the oil, helping with the lifting and hauling. He felt a rush of gratitude toward his old friend.

"I didn't do anything," Wes said. But Jack could see he was pleased to have his part in the rescue acknowledged.

"What's going to happen? Are you in trouble? Are civilians allowed to fly air force planes?"

Jack shrugged, corralling the nearly-too-heavy dog in his aching arms, and wobbled as he walked through the hangar.

"I don't know," he said. "And I don't care." He knew something about himself that he'd never known before. Jack Waters had flown solo. He smiled and hummed the tune from Basil's crazy song.

CHAPTER 26

"**H**ow come you never told us you could fly, Jackie?" asked Harold, when they met later at the cafeteria.

"It wasn't something I was ready to talk about."

"I bet your parents will be proud of what you did," said Angus. "I know I am."

"You don't know my mother."

"Too bad you aren't a couple of years older," said Angus.

"I for one am glad he isn't," said Harold.

"I've got bad eyes," said Jack. "I can't fly."

"You just did, boy," laughed Angus.

"After the war, who knows?" Harold got up. "Angus, drive this boy home. He needs to get cleaned up."

"We can take the dog and the doghouse in the back of the truck," Jack said. All the way into the village, Jack worried about his mother and the flying episode.

When they pulled up at the side of his house, he could see several heads through the window. Who was there? Mom and Dad should both be at the store.

His dad and Dr. McLeod came bounding out the back door, letting the screen door bang behind them. Both men gave Jack bear hugs. "Great job, lad!"

His mother and Mrs. McLeod came out and stood behind the men. Jack couldn't read his mother's face.

"I can explain," he said.

"How's Basil?" Mom asked calmly.

"I stopped by the infirmary. The station doctor says he'll be all right in a couple of days."

"You saved his life," said Dr. McLeod.

"This is getting to be a habit, son." Dad pounded Jack on his shoulder. "First Buddy and now Basil."

Hearing his name Buddy barked and pranced around the yard.

"I put the boiler full of water on the woodstove so you can get cleaned up," said his mother. She was talking about the big copper pot they used to heat bath water. "You look like heck." Jack couldn't help smiling. His mom was taking things awfully well.

"You're quite the clever fellow, Jackie Waters," said Mrs. McLeod.

His mother was picking roses by the door and looked

up. "We're pretty proud of him."

Jack's chest expanded. He'd been afraid she'd be really mad at him.

"Not many of us would have done what you did, Jack." Ivy brought Mary McLeod a few roses wrapped in tissue. "Take these home with you. They need water."

"We'll be going then," said Mrs. McLeod. "I brought over some fresh scones, Jack."

Ten minutes later Jack was sitting in the metal tub in the middle of the kitchen floor and it wasn't even Saturday night. Imagine having a bath in the middle of the week, he thought. It felt good, though, and he used the dipper to splash warm water over his head and washed his hair with soap. He slid down with his knees up and his torso submerged.

His parents had gone to the store and left him on his own with the plate of Mrs. McLeod's saskatoon berry scones and a pitcher of milk. He couldn't help it – he went over his flight from start to finish. Taking off over the spindly trees, soaring through the sky and experiencing the freedom that was flying. The surge of power over the machine and the elements, the wonder of space and the curve of the earth.

Even the scary bit at the end when he had trouble stopping the plane.

The water began to cool. Jack climbed out, towelled off, and called Buddy from his spot in the yard. The dog nosed the screen door open and padded into the kitchen. "It's your turn. But don't tell Mom I bathed you in the house. This bathtub is too heavy to haul outside."

He grabbed Buddy and put him in the tub, taking some dish soap to lather him up and the dipper to rinse him as the dog whined and shook. He looked quite annoyed, his eyes glaring. But soon he was released and bounded out the door and rolled on the grass. Buddy finally relaxed and curled in the sun by the caragana.

Jack cleaned up the kitchen, dumped the water and rinsed the tub, hanging it on its giant hook in the shed. He pulled on the fresh clothes his mother had laid out for him. He wolfed down four scones and two glasses of milk. Maybe he'd walk over to the store later and see how things were. But first he'd go into his room and stretch out for a few minutes. A wall of fatigue seemed to be surrounding him. It had been quite the day so far.

He'd drop into the infirmary with Wes and Cathy this evening.

Instead of a short nap, Jack slept most of the afternoon away.

asil was sitting up in bed in the infirmary, his head swathed in bandages. He had a pile of magazines and a plate of Cathy's brownies on his nightstand. Crickets chirped in the grass outside. Evening dew misted the window.

"So the Commanding Officer has been in asking for my report. The doctor told him to give me a day. Harold says 3828 needs a few repairs thanks to that wandering goose dancing with my propeller and getting sucked into the engine. Your boss is really proud of you, Jack. Feels like he gets some of the credit for training you in aircraft maintenance. After all, you got the plane going as well as flying it."

Jack blushed. He, Wes and Cathy sat in a row on the empty bed across from Basil.

"The doctor says I'd lost a lot of blood. You saved my life, young Waters. Who knows when anyone else would have come along?"

"Does the CO know about Jack?" Cathy asked.

"He wondered what happened. It wouldn't be the first civilian in a training plane."

Wes coughed. "I told Dad. He spread the word quickly."

"Everyone knows. No more secrets, Jackie." Cathy picked up a brownie absentmindedly. "Trevor would be proud of you, Jack."

"He took me up for a spin just before he died. He was a good flyer."

Basil sighed. Cathy fished in her pocket for a hankie.

"I've been thinking about my future," Jack said. "I'm going to university, and I'm going to learn how to make planes safer."

"Some day everyone will be taking plane rides, Jack," Wes said. "And you could help make that possible."

Jack grabbed a brownie. He didn't know what to say.

"How's your mother feel about it all?" Cathy asked.

"She said I could keep Buddy. We've won that war."

"Ivy liked Basil and Trevor more than anyone knows," Cathy said.

Jack didn't say what was in his mind: No one could have saved Trevor, maybe not even a safer plane. I'll never forget him, not in my whole life, not if I live to be a hundred. He looked away and blinked his eyes to keep the tears from falling.

"All the guys are leaving tomorrow," said Basil. "I have to stay put for a new more days. Blast it all anyway. A bloke needs company."

"Buddy and I will come after school."

"Brilliant."

"So will we," chimed in Wes and Cathy.

"I've got a few things to do," said Jack. "I'll see you guys tomorrow. Stop for me on your way to school, Wes. We'll go together."

"I'll be there too, my second day teaching." Cathy smiled. "The first one went just fine. I love the kids."

Jack was struck by the way Cathy looked now. There was new purpose in the way she moved. She'd grown up this summer. Losing people you cared about in war did something to your body and your heart.

Losing Trevor was harder than anything else in the world – losing a good friend, a person with so much talent and promise. Jack didn't feel sixteen. He felt years older than he'd felt in April before his first flight. He whispered a silent prayer for Sandy's safe return. The war still raged in Europe and the Far East.

Jack felt as if he had left childhood behind when he had flown in the sky over Cairn and when he stood with his father by the railroad tracks in Cairn. And finally, he'd felt older than the village as he visited the graveyard where Trevor and his Uncle Jack were buried, two young fliers who had never known each other. Both had played a part in Jack's life.

He left the McLeods with Basil and walked down the quiet corridor, out to where he'd leaned his bike against the fence. He stopped at the graveyard on his way home and paid his respects, told Trevor what had happened today, nodded in his uncle's direction and said hi to his grandparents.

ack cycled slowly back to Cairn. A gorgeous pink-and-lilac sunset lay before him. The sounds and smells of evening surrounded him. Gravel crunched under his tires, the roadside wolf willow and saskatoon bushes rustled in the breeze, the aroma of clover and sweet grass, of mown hay and alfalfa filled his nose. He was alone on the prairie. A bat whirred overhead.

One of the Boyles' trucks came barrelling along the road and slowed as it passed. Jimmy leaned out of the window and yelled, "You're a bloody hero, Jackie Waters. You sure had me fooled." He drove on, leaving Jack to eat his dust.

It tasted sweet.

Buddy was sitting in the backyard by the doghouse Cheese had built of scrap lumber and painted white. He bounded up to meet Jack and barked a fierce welcome. Jack crouched before the still soapy-smelling border collie. He wrapped his arms around Buddy's neck and buried his head on the dog's shoulder. It was good to be home.

HISTORICAL NOTES

No. 33 Elementary Flight Training School opened in November of 1941, outside Caron, Saskatchewan. It was one of nearly one hundred aerodromes and landing fields built in Canada during the first few years of the Second World War. It was part of the British Commonwealth Air Training Plan (BCATP). The province of Saskatchewan hosted 16 training facilities in both major cities and in numerous small towns across the prairies. The people responded warmly and generously welcomed student pilots and aircrew.

In the 1930s it became clear that airplanes and an air force would be a necessary part of any armed conflict with enemies like the Third Reich in Germany. That meant that young men had to be trained as pilots and crew, and soon. Discussions between the British and Canadian politicians, military leaders and bureaucrats went on for several years before the first schools finally were launched in 1940. Several men were instrumental in imagining the concept and working out the financial and functional details. For additional background on how the BCATP came about, read *Wings of Victory* by Spenser Dunmore or *Thousands Shall Fall* by Murray Peden. A good list of articles on the subject is available on the Internet under BCATP.

Noted Canadian historian J.L. Granatstein described the BCATP as the major Canadian contribution to the Allied War effort. Wing Commander Fred H. Hitchins thought that the air battle of Europe was won on the fields of the BCATP. Charles Gavan Power, Minister of National Defence for Air during World War II, maintained that the BCATP was the single most grandiose enterprise ever embarked on by Canada.

More than 131,000 aircrew members were trained. The BCATP trained young men from Great Britain, Australia, New Zealand and, of course, Canada. In all, 49,808 pilots, 29,963 navigators/observers, 15,673 air bombers, 18,496 wireless operators/air gunners, 1,913 flight engineers and 704 naval air gunners graduated from these training facilities.

More than 900 students, instructors and ground crew lost their lives during training. The community graveyard outside Caron and Caronport, Saskatchewan, with its ten well-tended military graves, is one of several across the country that holds the bodies of those young men who died in training accidents or crashes.

The De Havilland Moth

This plane was built in 1925 by Geoffrey de Havilland of England. It was recognized as an outstanding plane immediately. Several different engines and styles followed its creation. There followed the Gipsy Moth, the Cirrus, and the Tiger and Menasco Moth. Over the Moth's lifespan several modifications were made, like the enclosed canopy for Canadian climate, the metal fuselage, and other minor changes.

Most pilots in Canada in the nineteen thirties were trained in Moths. Moths were the most popular plane in the late twenties and thirties, used for short and long-distance flights. Amy Johnson flew a Moth from England to Australia in 1929. Tiger Moths were at first built in England, but in 1927 De Havilland of Canada was established to assemble and maintain Moths.

The Tiger Moth was used as a military training plane during World War II by the British Commonwealth Air Training Plan. It was used by the air forces of the UK, Australia, Brazil, Canada, Denmark, Iraq, New Zealand, Persia, Portugal, South Africa, Rhodesia and Sweden. After the war, Tiger Moths were sold to civilian companies and individuals. Many are still flying today and are collector's items.

You can find samples in most of the air museums across the country. Check them out. Remember that boys like Jack Waters and Trevor Knight (and some girls too) learned to fly in these small sturdy biplanes.

Nursing Sisters in the Second World War

Flo, Jack's older half-sister, served as a nurse overseas. How did these women sign up? How were they trained? What was it like? My curiosity was piqued. I searched on-line and discovered much information. I read several books. But the data lacked the human touch. Happily, I was introduced to retired army nurse Frances Ferguson Sutherland. She nursed overseas, both in England and in field hospitals in France and Belgium, and was glad to share her story with me. Approximately 5,000 women served as nursing sisters during the 1939 to 1945 conflict in the Army, Navy and Air Force medical corps.

In all, nearly 50,000 Canadian women served in the Armed Forces during World War II.

Personal Notes

The idea for this book had been lurking, as it were, for several years, waiting for the right moment. With Saskatchewan and Alberta celebrating their hundred years as part of the country in 2005, it seemed a good time to focus on one of the highlights of their history. The training of aircrew shouldn't be overlooked as one of the west's great contributions to the free world.

My husband Clair grew up in Saskatchewan, first in Arcola and then for five years in the village of Caron. Then he moved with his parents to southwestern Ontario. He was born in 1934, so he was about seven when the aerodrome at Caronport was built. He remembers the big trucks rolling through town, the yellow planes arriving by train and being flown to the airfield, then the RAF boys on a troop train in the middle of winter. It was pretty spectacular.

I started researching the BCATP several years ago. At the same time, I was playing with characters in my head. I knew I wanted to deal with the impact of the aerodrome on the village and its inhabitants. I was interested in the training and the planes and felt that if I had a protagonist of fifteen or sixteen I could do that better. So Jack Waters came to be.

I had an Uncle Jack who fought in the Second World War. Clair's mother's maiden name was Waters and the Waters family really did have a store in Caron. Grandpa Waters is buried in the Caron Cemetery close to the flyers. I wanted to honour them all, even though I never knew Clair's grandparents.

I have changed the name of the village, as I was not so much writing a history as I was writing a story within a historical time and place. For me the best way of remembering facts and figures is by hanging them on the lives and stories of real or imagined people.

In 2005, with a grant from the Alberta Foundation for the Arts, I travelled to Saskatchewan and spent a week camped near Mortlach. I visited the Moose Jaw Archives, which were really helpful. Clair took photos of the graves and the airport (It is now a bible college). I visited the Western Development Museum and the current airfield in Moose Jaw, and talked to old-timers and plane buffs. I took copious notes.

Since then I have reread all my notes, research materials and other books about the BCATP and written several drafts of the novel. As I prepare to send this off to Coteau Books, I pause to say thank you to all the people who helped with research, materials, family stories, and data. A reading list and more details about the BCATP will be available in the Teacher's Guide for this book.

Acknowledgements

I would like to thank all the people who helped with the research for this book. Several folk deserve special mention. Dr. Owen Cornish, my dentist's father, trained on Tiger Moths and flew in World War II. He read and critiqued the book in its early drafts. Dace Wiersma kept me in touch with her sister, graduate Paul Braid's widow Kathy. Paul's pilot's scarf, badges, log book, training notes and sketches informed me as I wrote. Gayle Simonson's father, Ken Rutherford, allowed me to interview him about his training and selection for navigator school in the early part of the 1940s. Gwen Molnar talked about being so young and joining up, and life in those times. Her husband George added insights as well. Frances Sutherland, a nursing sister in World War II, gave advice.

My husband, who had grown up close to a British Commonwealth Air Training Plan (BCATP) base outside of Moose Jaw, accompanied me as I toured and took photos at the old site, copied data from the Archives in Moose Jaw and visited the Western Development Museum, where Kate Johnson helped immensely. The hangars and museum in Edmonton and the planes in the Wetaskiwin museum inspired me. Denny May, Wop May's son, read the manuscript to check out technical details. Peter Woodbury, our son the pilot in Yellowknife, checked the flying scenes for me. I relied heavily on all these relatives and friends to keep my novel as historically and technically accurate as possible. Any errors are mine and I apologize.

I understand W. O. Mitchell used "Repete" as a nickname for a character in one of his early works. I liked it and I'm sure W.O. wouldn't mind that I used it too. He was a great writer. *Imitation is the sincerest form of gratitude.*

A grant from the Alberta Foundation for the Arts enabled me to go to Saskatchewan and do the research and then to stay home and work on this novel.

Finally, thanks go to the staff at Coteau Books for their continued interest in my work. Their editing, design and layout make this book a better book.

Mary Woodbury is the best-selling author of the young adult title *The Ghost in the Machine,* the Polly McDoodle Mystery Series, and *Jess and the Runaway Grandpa,* a finalist in the Silver Birch Young Readers Choice Award, and a Canadian Children's Book Centre "Outstanding Title of the Year". Other titles include *A Gift for Johnny Know-It-All, Brad's Universe,* and *Where in the World is Jenny Parker?* as well as adult collections of short stories and poetry.

Originally from Ontario, Mary lived in Newfoundland, New York and Italy before moving to Edmonton in the late 1970s. She lives there to this day.